HER DARKEST HOUR

A ROSEMARY RUN THRILLER

KELLY UTT

PROLOGUE

Eve Blackburn had just enjoyed one of the most exhilarating weeks of her life. She and her husband, Tim Fischer, had returned from a trip to the Florida Keys to celebrate their first wedding anniversary. They'd been trying to conceive ever since their honeymoon the year prior, and timing had lined up right during their stay in Islamorada. Eve was thrilled about the prospect of finally becoming pregnant. She longed to feel a baby moving around inside of her, to wear cute maternity clothes, and to pick out her child's name. She looked forward to it more than anything else. She was counting the days until she could take a home pregnancy test and confirm the happy news.

Eve came from a big brood, and her three older brothers already had spouses and kids of their own. Their parents, Wilder and Phoebe Blackburn, had instilled a strong sense of family in the kids that Eve wanted to replicate. Ty, Jake, and Holden were good brothers, having watched over their little sister with the utmost loving care. Eve had been doted on. Spoiled even. She had bloomed like a flower under the adoration showered upon her. Now that Eve and Tim were settled into married life and their cozy new home on Crickett Lane, she wanted to offer the same happy childhood to a baby they'd raise together, surrounded by the positive energy of their relatives.

In the Blackburn clan, loyalty to each other and to the family business was everything. Eve enjoyed her work as an event coordinator at Brambleberry Fields, her family's resort. She'd never dreamed about working anywhere else so, after graduating from college in Los Angeles with a degree in business, Eve had returned home to do her part. She eagerly awaited the day her little one would play in the sunshine on the property with his or her cousins and trot cheerfully behind Freckles, the farm dog.

At home in Rosemary Run on a bright February morning, Eve had recovered from jet lag and was ready to get back to her regular routine. Her family and friends would, no doubt, want to hear about her and Tim's trip. Life was good. Spring was coming, and the young couple had a lot to be happy about. Which is why it took Eve by complete surprise when she found herself waking up in a strange man's bed.

The shock was sudden and absolute. It moved through Eve's body like a bolt of lightning, causing her physical pain. As she rubbed her bleary eyes, she hoped what she was experiencing was nothing more than a bad dream. Her head felt foggy, and her limbs heavy. There was an incessant ringing in her ears. The room seemed to spin around her.

She told herself to close her eyes tightly, wishing with all her might that when she opened them a second time, she'd see Tim sleeping next to her instead of a stranger she didn't recognize.

1

E ve screamed. She couldn't help it. She heard the noise that came from her mouth, but it sounded far away. Foreign. It was as if she'd somehow left her body to watch what was happening from a distance. Time seemed to stand still as her blood pounded in her veins like an angry deluge.

Where am I?

She smoothed the red hair on the sides of her head in rhythmic motions, beginning at the crown and sliding downward until her fingers reached the wispy ends which cascaded around her bare bosom. She shrieked again, more sharply this time, frightened by her own nakedness. Clumsily, she grabbed a wad of sheet and flung it over top of herself.

How did I get here? I can't remember.

The man beside her lay still and silent, in a deep sleep. Eve thanked the heavens for that much.

Her motions quickly became more frantic. She felt somehow sped up. Reaching one hand for her hair again, she pulled on a clump of strands. Tearing and destroying her own scalp, she let her fingers do the work of the rage and confusion she felt inside. She pulled and ripped so hard that blood began to drip, reaching her shoulders.

Seeing the red drops as they rolled down her body and plopped onto the sheet was a surreal experience. Eve felt disconnected from the blood, like it was coming from someone else. Just like her screams.

What's wrong with me?

Escalating further, Eve thrashed and kicked, her naked flesh becoming exposed again. She flailed like a child having a temper tantrum. Her whole body got into the action, heaving and pushing. She was a bundle of terror, the intensity expressed in the only way her body knew how at that moment.

"What in the hell?"

The question came from the man in bed beside her. He was bleary-eyed, but alarmed by the dramatic scene unfolding around him.

Eve suddenly stopped screaming, the reality of her whereabouts flashing into focus. She looked at the man. He looked back, dumbfounded.

Eve opened her mouth to speak, but nothing came out. Instead, she picked herself up, clawing at the clothing strewn around the floor beside the bed. She wasn't sure it was hers. She wasn't processing. It didn't matter much if it was hers. Not right then. She needed to get out of there. And fast.

"Wait!" the man called.

Eve glanced at him, but didn't stop moving. With the balled up sheet and a few items of clothing in hand, she frantically scanned the room for an exit. A set of sliding glass doors led to a backyard patio. She set her sights, then rushed forward. Only she misjudged the situation and slammed into the cool glass.

Her head took the brunt of the impact. Eve saw stars and thought she might pass out. She stumbled around, reaching an arm out to steady herself. But there was nothing to grab onto. No one to help steady her.

How badly she wanted Tim. If he were there, he would cradle her in his embrace and tell her everything would be okay. It's what he always did when his wife got out of sorts. She needed him now. Oh, so much.

"Tim!" Eve cried as she fell to the floor, crashing down in an oppressive haze that refused to let her loose. "Tim! I need you. Come and get me, Tim."

As her awareness faded to black, Eve saw the strange man's feet in front of her. She couldn't fathom who he was or what he was doing there. She just wanted her husband. He would know what to do.

And then, everything went completely black.

2

***

It was a typical day on the resort grounds for Wilder and Phoebe. The sun shone brightly through the canopy of trees as the couple scattered cornmeal on the grass for their chickens. Mornings were cool this time of year, so the Blackburns offered their feathered friends a warm breakfast. When Wilder felt like it, he added boiled eggs and yogurt into the feed for a tasty treat. This morning's meal included both.

Wilder was a jovial guy. He could keep himself and those around him entertained in even the most difficult times. Visitors to Brambleberry Fields enjoyed the fun touches he added to their experience. In that spirit of fun, Wilder had named the hens on the property after legendary old Hollywood actresses. The most outgoing of the bunch were Greta Garbo, Audrey Hepburn, Grace Kelly, Elizabeth Taylor, and Marilyn Monroe. Neat wooden name plates hung from their coop along with custom portraits painted by Bea Earl, a local artist.

It was the kind of detail that made the resort special.

Greta was the leader of the pack. She was a pretty black and white with red around her beak. She ruled the roost when the rooster, Rock Hudson, wasn't around. She strutted proudly as the flock ate, surveying her domain.

"You sleep well?" Wilder asked the hen.

He talked to them like you would any pet.

"And how about you, Marilyn?" Wilder asked as she scrambled to get her turn in the spotlight.

Marilyn was a pretty golden color with the same red around her beak.

The girls were lookers, that was for sure.

Phoebe smiled as she watched her husband talk to the chickens. She loved Wilder fiercely. They had met when they were in college in their early twenties, and they fully intended to be one of those couples who die of old age on the same day while holding each other's hands. Their love was a sweet one, obvious to everyone who spent even a few minutes with them together.

"You're so silly," Phoebe said to her husband.

"What?" he replied, teasing. "Don't tell me you're jealous of all these beautiful girls who flock around me every morning."

"Ha!" Phoebe laughed. "You mean Greta and Marilyn?"

"Those are the ones. Beautiful girls."

"Should I be jealous?" Phoebe continued, smiling. "Are you trying to tell me something, Mr. Blackburn?"

Wilder laughed, then swung an arm around his wife and pulled her close. "You're my one and only, Mrs. Blackburn. Until my dying day. You know that." He kissed her on the top of the head as he gave her a squeeze.

"I know," she said softly. "It's still nice to hear."

"I'll tell you every day. I don't mind repeating myself," Wilder affirmed.

Marilyn clucked, apparently pleased.

The couple heard a pair of heavy footsteps behind them. They didn't have to turn and look to see who it was. They already knew.

"Morning, Holden," Wilder said.

The eldest of the Blackburn children worked full time as the resort's Director of Operations. He had gone all the way to New York City to earn an MBA from Columbia, only to return to the family business and put his knowledge to good use. He was a striking man with rugged good looks. He kept his blonde hair trimmed short. It fit with his tall stature and athletic physique. He looked every bit the part of a military colonel. Or a politician. Holden Blackburn seemed destined to be a leader.

"Morning, Mom and Dad," Holden said cheerfully.

Holden and his wife Lorelei had four young kids of their own. Three boys and a girl, just like their parents. They were doing their part to keep the Blackburn name going. They were a happy family. They were everything Wilder and Phoebe had hoped.

It was picture perfect.

"How are my grandbabies this morning?" Phoebe asked her son as he fell in step beside her and she put one arm around him. "Did they get pancakes and fruit in the shape of a face like they requested? Because I can have Doris make them some here at the restaurant if you like…"

"No need," Holden said. "They got them all right.

Lorelei made pancake faces a couple of hours ago. All four kiddos are full and happy. Off to school, as usual."

"Good," Phoebe said. "Lorelei is so good."

"She is," Holden affirmed. "That's why I married her."

Holden's relationship with his wife truly was a good one. Also like his parents.

Lorelei was from Jamaica. She and Holden had met in New York when they were both in graduate school. Trained as an attorney, Lorelei was taking time away from her career to be a stay at home mom while the kids were little. And it was a full house. Lorelei's own mother, Imogen Clarke, had been staying with the family as she recovered from hip surgery.

Holden and his parents walked quietly as a gentle wind blew across the hillside, rustling leaves and blades of grass.

The property sat on some of the most spectacular natural beauty in the entire Northern California wine country region. Brambleberry Fields was a gem for the town of Rosemary Run. Many of the tourists who came to town stayed at the Blackburn's resort, either at the inn or in one of the lake-side cottages.

"So, what's on the agenda for today?" Wilder asked his son.

Wilder and Phoebe were technically still in charge, but they let Holden head things up and make day-to-day decisions. He was perfectly capable. Even his siblings knew it. His leadership style was to rule by example. He motivated those around him because they wanted to please him.

"We're completely booked this weekend," Holden said. "We have the Springers coming in from Kansas City for their wedding on Saturday. They arrive on Thursday, so we have a few days to finish the prep."

"Are they using the wedding garden, or staying in the lodge?" Phoebe asked.

"The lodge only," Holden confirmed. "They didn't want to risk it being too cold outside. I think that was a wise decision."

"Agreed," Wilder said.

"I think the bride wanted to wear a strapless dress," Holden added. "Inside is definitely a safer bet."

Phoebe opened her eyes wide for dramatic effect. "Oh, yes," she said. "Inside! We wouldn't want complaints because the bride was freezing. We can't control the weather, after all."

They laughed together.

"Is your brother ready to brief us?" Phoebe asked.

"He is," Holden confirmed. "Both of them are. We'll go over everything in our morning meeting in about half an hour. Marcus, too. It's all hands on deck."

Jake Blackburn, Wilder and Phoebe's second son, handled events for the resort.

Ty Blackburn, their third son, handled the on-site winery, the wine tasting room and everything related. Ty's husband, Marcus Blackburn, handled food service and catering.

Brambleberry Fields truly was a family affair.

"When will Eve be back to work?" Wilder asked. "I haven't talked to her or Tim in several days. I trust their flight got in safely and that they had fun in the Keys."

"Yeah, I haven't heard from Sis in a while either," Holden confirmed. "I told her to take all the time she wanted. She always works hard for us. She deserves a break. I'm fine as long as she returns by the end of the week."

"Really?" Phoebe asked. "You don't worry about her?"

"Eh, not really. Tim looks after her."

"I know," Phoebe says. "But sometimes I wonder if Tim realizes what he's gotten into. You know? She's been better in the past few years since she's known him."

"We've told him, Phoebe," Wilder said. "That's all we can do."

Holden nodded his agreement.

"But, she's ours… I can't help but worry," Phoebe continued. "You know what I'm talking about. All the changes in her routine might cause a disruption…"

"I know," Wilder said softly to his wife. "She's our baby girl. Always will be."

"And my baby sis," Holden added.

"Tim will look after her," Wilder continued. "Let's focus on the resort. It's good to keep busy. No time to worry that way."

"I'm not sure that's how it works," Phoebe said, her forehead tightening as she thought about it all.

Holden and Wilder shared a knowing glance. They didn't want Phoebe to get worked up. They knew her concerns were valid, but they also knew there wasn't much any of them could do. Eve's troubles had begun in high school, more than ten years ago now. They had taken her for the best treatment money could buy. Her condition would be a lifelong challenge.

"Hey, let's focus on the positive," Holden said. "Back to business. Our employees are the best. They're filling in for Eve while she's away. We're good."

"I like the sound of that," Wilder said.

"Of course, you do," Phoebe said. "I love you for all your clowning, Wilder. But it can't fix everything."

Holden raised a hand to halt them, just before they entered the lodge.

"Look, Mom," he began. "We're going into a business meeting now. Remember that not everyone working here is family, even though it seems like it sometimes."

"I know," Phoebe said. "And you're our fearless leader."

"I try," Holden replied with a chuckle.

Wilder smiled big at his son. Ready to focus on the positive, as his son suggested.

"So, Mom," Holden continued. "If you want to call and check in with Sis and Tim, do it now. Out here. But the resort is doing just fine without Sis. I vote for giving them space. I'm sure they're fine."

Phoebe took a deep breath to calm herself. She tilted her head back, looking up at the sky. It was hard to be a parent of a child who had such challenges in life. It was hard to butt out. Her instincts told her to hover. To stay close, on high alert. The boys hadn't needed the same attention. They grew and developed normally, capable of handling themselves in the adult world. But Eve was different.

"Okay," Phoebe said. "You're right. You're both right. I said I'd back off and give her some space."

"Thank you," Holden replied. "Now, let's get down to business. Never a dull moment around here. Plenty to talk about."

Phoebe nodded, then followed her husband and son into the building.

3

The conference room was packed when Holden and his parents entered. Brambleberry Fields employed nearly six hundred people. Chefs, gardeners, a preservationist, a beekeeper, sommeliers, guest service men and women, concierge, housekeeping, corporate support, retail personnel, as well as grounds and maintenance teams. It was a large operation.

Key employees from each department participated in the weekly Monday morning meeting to touch base. This morning, a total of fifteen individuals sat at the ready, eager to do their part.

Jake, Ty, and Marcus were all present. They smiled and nodded to greet their elder family members.

The resort was casual and rustic, so no one wore suits and ties. But they were all dressed in the appropriate attire for their positions, many of them in neat, clean uniforms. They looked sharp.

"Hello, everyone," Holden said as he stepped to his

place at the head of the table and set his briefcase down. Phoebe and Wilder took their seats at his side.

"Hello… Good morning… Happy Monday…" the crowd bubbled in reply.

"You're all looking wonderful this morning. Your pride in our humble resort is showing," Holden said. "I might be biased, but I think we have the best team this side of the Mississippi… If not in all of America."

Holden's employees practically cooed in response, basking in the sincere praise from their boss. He had a knack for this.

Wilder winked at his son. He and Phoebe had built this business, after all. And they were pleased with Holden's handling of it. It was a dream come true for them, actually.

"Alright," Holden began, sitting down in his chair. "Let's get to it. We have a busy week. There's the usual weekday guests, the restaurant, wine tastings, the shop, the scheduled adventure activities plus live music in the barn on Friday night and the Springer wedding on Saturday. The wedding will have five hundred attendees. We all have to be on top of our game to ensure things go off without a hitch."

The group laughed at the choice of words, winking and smiling at each other.

"Or maybe I should say, *with* a hitch," Holden corrected, chuckling.

A few good-natured comments followed, the group relaxing into their familiar rapport.

Little did the Blackburn family know, one of their own was in great peril. Phoebe was right to worry about Eve.

The baby of the bunch needed them now more than ever. But no one knew it. No one but the mystery man who had shared Eve's bed.

"Who wants to give their weekly update first?" Holden asked the team.

Jake raised his hand, ever the obedient little brother striving to make Holden proud. "I will."

Wilder nodded his approval and winked at his boys. He was proud of the way they worked well together. He often thought about his legacy and what he and Phoebe would leave to their children. Wilder wanted his kids to enjoy running the resort. He never wished for them to feel trapped or obligated. Not on his account.

"Then you're up," Holden said to Jake. "Let's hear from our Director of Events."

Jake stood up, a few inches shorter than Holden but every bit as handsome. He had the same blonde hair, but blue eyes instead of Holden's brown. Jake could command a room in his own right. He had excelled in undergraduate business school in San Francisco, then a graduate program in hospitality management. He was well prepared for his job.

"Thanks, bro," Jake began, enjoying the camaraderie. "We're in good shape for the Springer wedding, assuming everyone does their part. As most of you know, this is one of the larger weddings we've hosted at Brambleberry Fields. We only do four or five this size each year. You'd be surprised how much more difficult it is to host five hundred people as compared to two hundred and fifty."

"I hear that," Holden commented.

"Exponentially harder," Jake continued. "Proper prior

planning is everything. You all remember the seven Ps, right?"

They did. The group recited them together.

"That's correct," Jake confirmed. "Proper prior planning prevents piss poor performance."

Holden laughed. Jake was a little more direct and less diplomatic than he was with employees, but it worked for him.

"Anything we should watch out for?" one of Jake's assistants asked, his face eager.

"Good question," Jake replied. "I like questions. There are no wrong questions."

The assistant nodded, agreeing with Jake and appreciating his enthusiasm. "Yes, sir."

"Honestly, we're in pretty good shape," Jake said. "We have our processes refined and we know how to host a flawless, memorable event. The biggest concern right now in my mind, is the weather."

The group mumbled and chatted amongst themselves. They had heard the forecast.

"That's right," Marcus inserted.

He and Ty had only been married for two years, but it felt to the Blackburns like Marcus had always been a part of the group. He was a welcome addition, along with the couple's baby girl, Bethany.

Little Bethany was born with the help of an egg donor and surrogate. It was one of the times in Wilder and Phoebe's lives when they were tremendously grateful for the financial abundance that made such a miracle of modern medicine accessible to their son and his husband. Ty and Marcus chose an egg donor with rich brown skin and strong features like Marcus'. With the donor's egg fertilized by Ty's sperm, Bethany's skin tone and features looked as if she was a genetic mix of her two dads. Strangers couldn't tell which of her dads was the biological one. That suited Ty and Marcus just fine. Bethany was *theirs*. Biology be damned.

"Go ahead, Marcus," Holden prompted. "Let's hear from our Director of Food and Beverage. What do you know?"

Marcus had attended culinary school in Paris, then returned to his native California for the same hospitality management graduate program Jake attended. It was through a friendship with Jake that Marcus met and fell in love with Ty, the younger Blackburn brother.

It all seemed genuinely meant to be.

Marcus cleared his throat before he began. He was an outstanding Director of Food and Beverage, but he wasn't as confident as the Blackburns when it came to speaking up in a business meeting.

"I heard from some of my food suppliers, then I checked the local news. Meteorologists are predicting a rare snowfall overnight tomorrow. If it happens, things will come to a halt around here. Wine country people don't much know what to do about the white stuff."

"I hear that," Holden remarked. "This isn't New York City, that's for sure."

Everyone chuckled nervously.

Any disruption to the routine would throw a wrench in the works. It could mean delays, unhappy guests, bad reviews, and a slew of other unfortunate events that might set the family business back in a big way.

"That's what I'm hearing, too," Jake confirmed. "I don't know how much stock I should put in the weather report. Snow is so rare this low."

"This low?" Jake's assistant asked, for clarification.

"Yeah, buddy. It's rare at this low elevation. It happens often enough at higher elevation in the mountains."

Ty piped up, adding his perspective as Wine Director. "Surprisingly enough, snow is great for grapevines, as long as it doesn't last into spring."

"Huh," Holden said, intrigued. "It's been so long since we had snow around here that I scarcely remember."

"You were a kid!" Phoebe said. "Of course you don't remember much. But it happens sometimes."

Holden smiled politely, reserving his comment. He wanted to stick to business and avoid mention of his childhood. "So, it sounds like the biggest concern is disruption to our usual routines, specifically disruptions with our suppliers. Do I have that right?" he asked.

Jake, Marcus, and Ty agreed.

"Well then, that's our challenge this week," Holden confirmed. "We prepare ahead as much as we can. And then we work hard to take good care of our guests if the storm comes our way. Just like we always do."

Reassured, the team continued their meeting, launching into specifics about what they were working on and strategizing on how to cope with a potential disruption.

Holden didn't even hear his phone ding when the text came in. It was from Victoria Baker, Eve's longtime best friend.

4

———

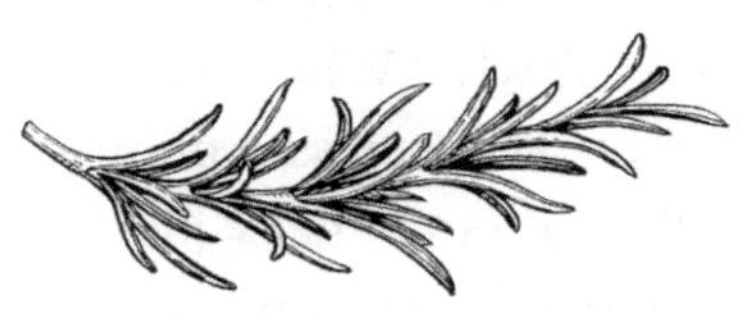

"Something's wrong." Victoria was breathless as she said it.

Holden had stepped outside to call her in response to her **9-1-1** text. Victoria hadn't provided any more detail.

Holden hated to leave the meeting. What else was he supposed to do? He knew that Victoria was prone to dramatics, but she was a good friend to his sister. She had earned the Blackburn family's respect over the years.

"What do you mean? What is it?" Holden asked, talking quietly so as not to be overheard.

The conference room had mostly glass walls. Phoebe peered out at her son, her face a mix of surprise and knowing. It was sometimes eerie how much Phoebe understood without being told. She had an intuition that none of the rest of them understood. Only Lorelei's mom, Imogen, claimed to grasp Phoebe's apparent extrasensory perception. Imogen claimed that such powers were respected in Jamaican culture.

"It's Eve," Victoria confirmed, her voice insistent.

"What about Eve?" Holden asked. He was quickly growing impatient. If something was wrong with his sister, he didn't want Victoria to beat around the bush.

"I don't know, exactly," the young woman said. "But *something* is wrong."

Holden rolled his eyes, frustrated.

"Okay," he said slowly. "What makes you think so?"

Victoria sighed heavily into the phone.

"I can't reach her. And that's just for starters. Have you seen her social media accounts the past few days?"

"No," Holden said. With a wife, a live-in mother-in-law recovering from surgery, four young kids, and a resort to run, he didn't spend a lot of time on social media… A fact lost on Victoria. "I'll look now."

"It's bizarre," Victoria continued. "None of it seems right. I think she's off her meds again."

Victoria was a patient coordinator at the drug and alcohol rehab unit in the local hospital. She was still in school part time to earn a degree in counseling so that she could do more than schedule appointments. She was a bright girl, but she knew just enough to think she was better informed than she actually was. Holden often thought that Victoria needed five or six years to mature, and then would be a solid resource. As of right now, she just wasn't developed enough. She was green. Most of all, Victoria wasn't qualified to truly understand Eve's condition. Not as a professional, anyway.

Holden put his mobile phone on speaker while he flipped through his sister's Facebook feed, then Instagram.

"Wow," he muttered. "I think you may be right."

"You don't have to sound so surprised," Victoria replied.

"I don't mean it like that," he said.

As the oldest of the Blackburn siblings, Holden often ended up an enforcer. He was the one who had to tell Eve and Victoria to go to sleep when they tried to stay up too late at middle school slumber parties. He was the one who had to intercept them when they tried to sneak out of the house the weekend in high school that Wilder and Phoebe were out of town. And he was the one who had to pick them up when Eve got out of sorts and Victoria didn't know how to handle her.

"Have you tried Tim?" he asked.

"Of course, I did. No answer. His phone goes right to voicemail."

"Huh," Holden mused. "That's strange. He's the reliable one."

"I know," Victoria agreed. "I think his phone is turned off."

Holden continued to look through Instagram, trying to make sense out of what he was seeing. Eve had posted vacation photos from the Keys up until four days ago. Then she went silent for two days, which was highly unusual for her. *Especially* since she had been on vacation.

It had seemed like she was enjoying Florida, based on all the bikini-clad pictures she had shared. Both Eve and Tim were shown smiling from ear to ear as they fed iguanas, swam in the ocean, and rode bikes around the islands.

After two days of social-media silence, Eve had posted a flurry of quotes about life being unfair. That was the strangest part of it all. Holden knew his sister sometimes got down on herself, but he'd never seen her post her negative self-talk online.

"What do you make of this?" he asked Victoria.

Holden glanced back at the conference room, and could see Phoebe's level of alarm rising. It looked like she was about to get up and come out into the hall to find out what was happening.

He wasn't sure what he'd tell his parents. There wasn't anything to tell... yet.

Victoria sighed again, more distressed. "I don't know, Holden. That's why I got in touch. But I'm telling you… Something is wrong. I think it might be something bad."

"Okay," he replied simply.

"I think we need to find her," Victoria continued. "Like, right away."

Holden glanced back at the conference room and looked into his mom's eyes. He scolded himself for not listening to her earlier. Nothing at the resort mattered. Not really. Not if Eve was in danger.

"Give me a little while," he said. "I'll see what I can figure out."

"What should I do in the meantime?" Victoria asked.

"Keep trying to reach Sis. And watch social media for clues. Otherwise, wait for me to get back to you. I promise I'll let you know as soon as I hear something."

Victoria agreed, then hung up the phone, just as Phoebe arrived to confirm her suspicions about her daughter.

"Holden," Phoebe began, getting right to the point. "I

know it's Eve. Something is wrong, isn't it? Who was on the phone?"

Holden put a hand on his mom's shoulder, looking her in the eye. He thought her face looked weathered, suddenly more sunken and tired than usual. He knew it was a great burden to parent a child who could never be completely on their own. A child who would always need looked after. He said a silent prayer of thanks that all four of his kids had avoided whatever misguided gene Eve had been dealt. Though he couldn't be sure that it wouldn't rear its ugly head when they grew older.

"Mom," Holden began. "Let's not jump to conclusions."

"Boy," Phoebe scolded. "You may be in charge at the resort, but don't you forget who you're talking to. Don't you try to manage me."

"Fine," Holden said. "I'm sorry."

He didn't mean any disrespect to his mom. Eve's situation was difficult. None of them really knew how to help. They each tried in their own way, to the best of their abilities. But they often fell short.

"Who was on the phone?" Phoebe asked insistently, her head angled forward with interest.

"Victoria."

Phoebe took a breath to steady herself. "And what did she say?"

"That she can't reach Sis."

"And?"

"And what?" Holden tried.

"That was an awful long conversation to say only that she couldn't reach Eve, Holden. What else?"

Holden sighed now, glancing back into the conference room. Several team members had caught on to what was happening in the hall. They looked worried, too.

"And she thinks Sis' behavior on social media seems odd."

"How so?"

Holden proceeded to explain what was strange about Eve's posts, then he handed over his phone to show her.

Phoebe took one look at Eve's Instagram feed, then motioned for Wilder to step out of the meeting and join her. He did, followed by Jake, Ty, and Marcus.

If a family emergency was occurring, they all wanted to do their part.

"What?" Wilder said as the six of them huddled together, eyes wide.

They knew without saying that it was probably about Eve. It was almost always about Eve.

"She's in trouble," Phoebe said. "I knew it. I felt it earlier."

"What do you know?" Wilder asked, aiming his question at Holden. He knew he could count on his eldest son to keep a level head.

Holden repeated the explanation he had provided Phoebe, then they each pulled out their own smartphones to get a look at Eve's social media. They agreed that something was up.

Holden and Wilder looked at each other. They shared the same personality type, one that hinged on logic and process. Theirs was completely different than Phoebe's intuition-based tendencies. Jake, Ty, and Marcus knew to hang back and wait for one of the others to take the lead.

They were ready to do their parts, but didn't want to overstep.

"Mom," Holden said, deferring to the matriarch of the family. "What do you want to do?"

Phoebe nodded, glad for the chance to do things her way. "We start with the basics. Wilder, call the phone carrier and see if they'll give you information on its last known whereabouts."

"On it," he said. "I'm glad Eve is still on our family plan. I'm not sure they would talk to me otherwise."

"Holden," Phoebe continued. "Call Tim's mom, Margaret, in Phoenix. Find out when she last heard from them."

"But…" Holden blurted. "I don't think Tim keeps in touch…"

"I know, and I don't care," Phoebe continued. "Find out what she knows."

"Fine, done."

"Jake," Phoebe continued. "Call Tim's boss at the environmental advocacy firm. Find out if they've heard from him, and when they expect him back in the office."

"Okay, got it," Jake replied, marching to a quiet area to make the inquiry.

"And… Everyone," Phoebe called out loudly. "See if you can get their flight number. They were scheduled to return on a direct flight from Miami to San Francisco."

Ty and Marcus hugged each other, rattled by the fear for Ty's little sister.

"Mom, what can we do?" Ty asked.

Phoebe put her hand on her head as she paced, thinking.

"Um…" she said, uncertain. "I know. Go to their house. See if it looks like anyone has been there. Talk to their neighbors. Find any clues you can as to their whereabouts."

"Will do," Ty said.

"And the meeting?" Marcus asked reluctantly.

"Forget the meeting," Phoebe replied. "We have to get our girl. She needs us. Now go!"

They scattered along with the others, all following instructions as they worked to find Eve.

Phoebe leaned her back against a wooden wall, then let her body slide down into a sitting position. She was overwhelmed. Her legs threatened to fail her. But she was determined. The Blackburns looked out for one another.

They would find Eve and bring her home safely. Just like they had done before.

5

____

Eve's vision was grainy, but functional as it began to come back. Her mind whirled. She was unsure of everything.

Where am I?

It was as if her mind had played tricks on her. It was unreliable. Defective. She silently cursed. She wondered why she couldn't have been blessed with a healthy, in-tact brain like her older brothers. Things came easy for Holden, Jake, and Ty by comparison. Eve wondered if they knew how good they had it.

Daylight made its way through a large glass door.

Oh, yeah. The glass. I smacked right into it.

Eve sat up slowly, taking stock of her surroundings. Her head hurt something awful. She had banged it good. She wondered if she needed to see a doctor.

I'll just get my phone and call for a doctor… Except… Oh, no.

In a sudden jolt of terror, Eve remembered her circumstances. The strange man. The strange room. Her nakedness. The drops of blood.

In what might have been an act of self-preservation, her mind left the details fuzzy. Eve couldn't quite remember all that she'd perceived. She wasn't even sure what day it was.

Think.

In a wave of sadness, Eve remembered Tim, and again wished he was there to help her. He'd know what to do.

The emotion felt like a tsunami, sucking everything up only to churn it up and spit it back out in a volume that was nothing short of overwhelming. Eve felt like she was drowning underneath it. Like she was flailing and scrambling for air. But relief wouldn't come. It was as elusive as the ocean surface.

"I need my husband," Eve said, to no one in particular. "Hello?"

Silence greeted her, a cold and unforgiving reply.

"Tim. Tim Fischer. I need to get in touch with him," she tried, raising her head up as high as she could against the oppressive pounding.

Still nothing. No response.

Until a man's voice called out from another room.

"Are you awake?" he asked.

"Tim?"

"Are you okay?"

"Tim?! Is that you?" Eve cried. "Come and get me, Tim."

Silence.

"Tim? Please." Eve became increasingly desperate. "I think I need to go to the doctor. I'm hurt."

A male figure appeared in the doorway. Eve could

barely make out the details of his physique. He was about as tall as Tim. Something wasn't right about him though.

"Tim?" Eve tried again. "You look different. Are you wearing different clothes?"

She reached a hand up against her bruised forehead, blood dried against her skin.

"Eve? Are you okay?"

She startled when she heard her name. Tim called her E. Never Eve. Not once. Not even in front of other people. Always E.

Why would Tim call me that? I don't understand.

"Tim, you don't call me that," she mumbled. "Why are you acting weird? Come on, honey. I think I need a doctor. Come and get me."

The male figure moved closer, blocking out the sunlight. He reached a hand towards Eve. She sat still, feeling frozen in place. She still didn't know what to do. She still wasn't sure what was going on.

Maybe this is a dream. Yes! That's it. I'm dreaming. This is a bad dream.

"I think maybe you had a bad trip," the strange man said.

"Oh, no, Tim," Eve replied, shifting focus again. "We had a great trip. You remember! It was the best trip ever. Until…"

Eve began to sob, big tears rolling out of her eyes. She pulled her knees up to her chest and rocked back and forth, curling into a fetal position.

"What are you talking about?" the man asked. "I meant a drug trip. Did you take something last night?"

Eve looked up at him, his face still nothing more than a dark shadow. She couldn't make out his features.

"What?" she asked. "I don't…"

"Something is wrong," he said. "This is whack. I've got to call someone."

"Yes!" Eve replied. "Call me a doctor, Tim. I think I hurt my head. And I can't think straight. Something is wrong. You're right."

"Do you have any ID on you?" the man asked, the concern evident in his voice. "Who should I call?"

"Tim!" Eve screamed as she continued to cry and rock, gripping her knees even tighter. "Tim! Stop acting weird. Come get me, Tim!"

The man moved backward, and the sunlight poured in again, assaulting Eve's senses.

"It's bright!" she screamed. "Too bright. Make it stop. Help me, Tim. Please."

"How about a phone?" the man asked. "You probably have your contacts saved in there. Do you have a phone on you?"

Eve shrieked now. She couldn't understand why Tim was asking such strange questions. She just wanted to go to the doctor so he could fix her up. Then she wanted to go home. She wanted to get into her bed with her husband and forget that any of this had happened.

Maybe Tim knew where her pills were. Eve thought he probably did.

"My pills, Tim! They will help."

Tears soaked Eve's body, and she was once more aware of her nakedness. But she wasn't upset this time. It was only Tim, after all. She didn't have to cover up around him.

"I don't have pills," the man's voice said. "I'm sorry. Do you want me to call anyone?"

Eve looked up at the man, his face finally coming into focus. To her horror, it wasn't Tim after all. This man looked completely different from Tim.

Afraid and confused, Eve screamed as loud as she could for as long as she could until, finally, the man left her alone in the room. Exhausted, she dozed off to sleep in a haze as she struggled to stay lucid.

6

The Blackburns made their calls from various nooks and crannies in the lodge on the Brambleberry Fields property. When they had bits of information to share, they reconvened to discuss.

"Margaret hasn't heard from Tim in weeks," Holden said, his breathing heavy from worry. "She didn't even know they were in the Keys. She said he called to wish her a Merry Christmas, but they didn't talk long. Nothing seemed out of the ordinary."

"Damn," Wilder said, placing a hand on Phoebe's shoulder. "Not much luck on my end either. A customer service rep at the phone company walked me through the process of tracking Eve's last recorded location and accessing her call records. She used her phone normally up until four days ago. Her last known location was Islamorada, Florida. After that, nothing. It's like her phone has been completely turned off."

"I wonder how she was posting on social media in the days since," Holden said. "Maybe her battery died?"

"No," Phoebe said. "Tim would have called or texted. Or Eve would have called using his phone."

"Maybe that's how she got on social media," Holden offered. "Tim's phone. But I tried it and it goes right to voicemail, just like Victoria said."

"Jake? Any luck?" Holden asked as his brother hung up a call on his mobile phone and approached.

"I'm afraid not," Jake replied. "I spoke with Tim's boss. He was reluctant to share any information, but finally told me that Tim had been scheduled to return to work this morning. He didn't show up. And they haven't been able to reach him either."

Phoebe's hands shot up to her mouth. This piece of information alarmed her most of all.

Tim loved his job. He worked with a sustainability certification program for vineyards and wineries in the area. He had a PhD in environmental science and enjoyed every minute of both his studies and his career. It wasn't like him to disappear. He was as reliable and dependable as they come.

"Phoebe, take it easy," Wilder said. "Let's not jump to conclusions."

But Phoebe didn't want to take it easy. She couldn't. Her daughter needed her. Maybe Tim did, too. He wasn't close to his own family. It wasn't like he had bad feelings towards them. They just weren't a particularly close family. But he had become integral to the Blackburns. They were the big, close family Tim had always wanted. If he was in trouble, Phoebe intended to do right by Tim, the same as Eve.

The meeting was still going on in the conference

room, and the remaining team members were clearly very concerned about what was happening with the Blackburn family. A junior associate of Holden's had stepped up to take over the meeting. But no one could focus.

Within minutes, the meeting apparently dismissed and colleagues came streaming out of the conference room. They made their way to the Blackburns' sides, offering kind words and pledges to hold down the fort while things got sorted out. They were a close group. And nothing quite like this had happened before. At least, not as far as the employees knew. The family had successfully kept their personal business private until now.

Ty and Marcus rang Phoebe's phone, calling to report from Tim and Eve's house. With the ringer on full volume, the sound cut through the noise. The crowd cleared, giving the family the space they needed.

"Ty, son?" Phoebe answered, putting the phone on speaker so Wilder, Holden, and Jake could hear. "Are they home?"

"Mom," Ty said, sounding concerned. "They're not. But they're supposed to be."

"What do you mean?" Wilder asked, becoming alarmed now along with his wife. "How do you know they were supposed to be?"

"Because we talked to their neighbor, Mona," Marcus added, joining his husband.

"Yeah," Ty continued. "She was watching the house for them. They told her they'd be back yesterday afternoon. But they never came home. She tried to call them also. No answer."

"Oh, my God," Phoebe said.

"I don't know, Mom," Holden tried. "Maybe they decided to stay an extra day in the Keys. Or maybe they decided to hang out in San Francisco a while before driving home to Rosemary Run. You know… extend the fun a while longer."

"Without telling Tim's boss?" Jake added.

"Holden, I hear what you're saying," Phoebe said. "But the knot in the pit of my stomach tells me that isn't what happened. We need to call the police."

"Wait," Ty inserted.

"Wait for what?" Phoebe asked, exasperated.

"Mona has a key," Ty replied. "She offered to give it to us. I don't want to overstep and invade their privacy…"

"Screw privacy!" Phoebe exclaimed. "Stay put. We'll be right there."

They practically ran to the parking lot, gravel crunching underneath their feet. The sound seemed to drown out everything else. They were one unit, marching into battle together. Even though they were all scared, their shared mission was a comfort. They were there in solidarity. Ready to do whatever was necessary to take care of their own.

"I'll drive," Holden offered.

Without even answering, the group of them raced to his SUV and piled inside. There was no time to waste.

They all knew that calling the police was the next logical step. If they couldn't find clues in the house, they'd have no choice. And they didn't want to think about a police investigation. Those rarely had happy endings. Any hope of this turning out okay had to come soon, or it probably wouldn't come at all.

The heaviness of it sat on top of the family like a lead weight as they made their way to Tim and Eve's house at 242 Crickett Lane.

Holden and Jake hadn't even had a chance to call their wives yet. This was happening fast. It was not how any of them had intended to spend their Monday.

Ty and Marcus were waiting on the porch when they arrived, standing up with the key in hand. A solemn-looking elderly woman sat nearby on an Adirondack chair next to the front door.

"That must be Mona," Holden said. "Anyone met her before?"

"No," they replied in unison.

"Alright, then," Holden said. "Let's be extra nice to the lady. She's doing us a favor here."

Wilder and Jake agreed. Phoebe sat stoically, in an almost trance-like state.

"Mom?" Holden asked. "You okay?"

She nodded ever so slightly. She was in her own world. It seemed to her sons that Phoebe might have been meditating or somehow tapping into her extrasensory powers. The boys often gave their mom grief over her mysterious and witchy ways. But in this situation, no one minded. They needed all the help they could get.

Slowly, Phoebe stood, helped by Holden. He led his mom to the front door of his little sister's house as Wilder and Jake followed closely behind.

"Mona," Holden said as he reached out his hand to shake hers. "We can't thank you enough for your help. I trust Ty and Marcus explained the situation?"

"They did," Mona confirmed. "Nice boys, those two... You are a nice family. I hope Tim and Eve are okay."

"Thank you," Phoebe mouthed as Ty used the key to open the front door of the home.

They hurried inside, unsure of exactly what they were looking for, but compelled to find it nonetheless.

"What's the plan?" Jake asked.

Again, Holden deferred to Phoebe. "Mom?"

She nodded her thanks. She knew that Holden was capable of taking the lead. And she knew he was inclined to. But Eve was her child. She appreciated the fact that Holden was letting her take charge.

"Split up," Phoebe instructed. "Look for any clues about their whereabouts... schedules, itineraries, passwords. We're past the point of being concerned about privacy. We have to find them. They'll forgive us. Once they're safe. I know they will."

"Okay," Holden said, heading to his sister's home office to examine her computer.

"Got it," Wilder said. He was becoming more and more shell-shocked as events continued to unfold. He appreciated his wife's ability to remain calm under this kind of pressure. Especially because he was beginning to fall apart. "I'll look around for an itinerary. Or plane tickets. Or whatever..."

Jake, Ty, and Marcus went into three different rooms, scouring the place for anything that might be useful.

For her part, Phoebe sat on the living room sofa and closed her eyes. She visualized success, seeing in her mind's eye a piece of paper that would provide them some key information. It wasn't long until such a paper was located.

"I've got something," Marcus said from Tim and Eve's bedroom. He rushed downstairs to tell the others.

"What did you find?" Holden asked.

"It's their flight schedule from the airline. A print out was folded up on Eve's nightstand. She must have left it behind accidentally. Thank goodness."

"Bless you," Phoebe said to Marcus, grasping one of his hands and giving it a squeeze. "What does it say?"

Marcus set the paper down on the coffee table for everyone to see. "It shows their return flight landing in San Francisco yesterday afternoon, just like Mona said."

"Then what in the hell?" Wilder mused. "Where are they?"

"We need to find out whether they were on that plane," Holden asserted. "That's our next step."

"Will the airlines divulge that information?" Ty asked.

"I don't know," Holden said. "But we're about to find out. It's the best piece of information we have to go on right now."

"Anyone have connections that could get us that kind of access?" Wilder asked. "Any airport or airline connections? Now's the time to use them."

"I do," Phoebe said, to her family's surprise.

"Really?" Wilder asked his wife. "Who?"

"Monique Jackson," she replied. "An old friend from school. I haven't talked to her in years, but we're friends on Facebook. She works at the San Francisco airport. She'll tell me if they were on that plane or not."

"Good!" Holden said.

"Do it," Wilder urged. "Right away."

Phoebe fumbled with her phone as she tried to hurry. "I have to contact her through Facebook. I don't know how to do it any other way."

"Fine," Holden said. "In the meantime, everybody, keep searching the house. We might find something else that could help."

7

When Eve woke again, she felt better. Different. Her head was clear. It still hurt, but she felt like herself again. She could think straight. Mostly.

"You're awake," the strange man said.

He was seated in a chair beside Eve's bed. She jumped, but quickly collected herself as the memory of him came back.

"Yes, hello," she said timidly.

"I'm glad you're up," he replied. "I've been worried about you. Real worried."

"No need," Eve said. "I'm fine."

The man looked at her curiously.

Eve could make out the fine details of his face now. He appeared to be older than her by a few years, but in her general age range. He had brown skin, darker than her own. He looked Hispanic. He was an attractive man with slick black hair and big brown eyes. Eve felt a twinge between her legs and suddenly had a memory of this man being inside of her.

What have I done?

"Eve, right?" he asked gently.

"How do you know my name?" Eve asked as she pulled the sheet up tightly under her neck. It was stained and bloody. Visions of what had happened were coming back to her. She felt embarrassed. She hated for anyone to see her when she got like that.

"You told me your name last night. Remember?"

Eve squinted her eyes as she worked to bring the memory forward.

Oh, right. The bar. The dancing. The drinking.

"Yeah, I guess I do," she replied. "What's your name?"

"Saul."

"Okay, Saul," Eve replied. "Nice to meet you."

"You, too," he returned. "Eve… What's your last name?"

Thank God I didn't tell him that.

"Um… I don't know."

"You don't know?" Saul asked, taking a sip from a blue coffee mug with the outline of a bird on the front.

"Say," Eve began, "is that coffee? Do you have any more?"

"Sure," Saul replied, then he left the room to retrieve a second mug of the warm beverage.

Eve kicked into high gear once he was gone, scrambling to piece together her belongings and get herself dressed. She was disturbed to realize that her phone and her wallet were missing. A vague memory of what had happened to them tried to present itself, but it was too painful. Eve pushed it down. Locked it away.

She managed to get her shirt and bra on successfully.

She was pulling her stretchy jeans over her hips when Saul returned with the coffee. Her underwear weren't anywhere in sight, a fact that concerned Eve.

"Here," Saul said as he handed her a mug. It was red, with the same bird design on the front. They must have been part of a matching set.

"Who else is here?" Eve asked, taking a sip of the coffee. It was bitter. She should have asked for cream and sugar.

"No one," Saul said. "Only the two of us. Why?"

"Just wondered," Eve replied.

Saul leaned back in his chair. He had a gentle demeanor about him. Eve felt safe with him. If he were going to hurt her, he could have done it while she was out.

"So, back to your name," he tried. "What's your last name? We should probably call someone to look after you."

Eve didn't want Saul to know her last name. And she didn't want him to call anyone. She thought her family would be disappointed in her when they found out. She wanted to avoid that ugliness if at all possible. She was disappointed enough in herself.

"What's your last name?" she asked, turning it around on him.

"Milton. Saul Milton."

That was easy.

"Nice to meet you, Saul Milton."

"You, too. Eve…?"

She covered her face with one hand. "I'm shy, okay. I don't want to say my last name. Not yet. Think of me as Eve Smith if it helps."

Saul squinted his eyes and tilted his head again, trying to size her up. He didn't know what to make of Eve. He'd never seen anything like this.

"Okay… I guess," he said. "For now. But I really think we should call someone. I'll bet you have someone who is worried about you right now. Parents? A roommate?"

Remembering Tim, Eve glanced down at her ring finger. Her wedding band was gone. A jolt of electricity shot through her as she realized. And not the good kind of electricity. This was physically painful, as if she'd actually received a shock.

"See… that right there…" Saul continued. "That reaction tells me there is *someone*. Let me call them. Please."

Eve shook her head adamantly. "No," she asserted, standing up from the bed with her purse in hand. "I'm a grown woman. I don't need a babysitter."

Saul stood up, too. "I don't mean any disrespect," he said. "I want to help."

"Saul, we slept together last night, right?"

"We did."

"We left Wingman's Pub together, right?"

"That's right," Saul confirmed, unsure where this line of questions was going.

"Was I woman enough for you then?"

Eve stepped close to Saul, her breath warm on his neck. She traced a line from his sternum down to his belt buckle with her fingertips.

"Last night was amazing," he said. "But you don't seem okay…"

"Hush," Eve said as she raised a finger up to his lips.

She remembered those lips in another flash. They had felt good on her body. "How about you show me to a bathroom where I can get cleaned up and we'll spend the day together?"

Saul tilted his head again, considering her proposition.

"What?" Eve asked when he paused. "You have somewhere else to be?"

"No," he replied quickly. "I'm off work today. Nowhere else to be."

"Then it's settled," Eve said. "The bathroom?"

Saul pointed. "Down the hall. Second door on the left."

"Give me twenty minutes," Eve said, winking seductively. "Maybe, if you're lucky, you'll get a repeat of last night."

8

In Saul's bathroom with the door securely shut and locked, Eve came undone. She paced nervously across the black and white tile floor, pulling at her red hair again as tears streamed down her face.

Eve felt stuck. Trapped. And helpless. She had no driver's license. No phone. No money. She didn't even know where she was.

Her only option was to call her family… assuming Saul would let her use his phone like he suggested. But Eve couldn't face her family.

Her parents would overreact like they always did. Holden would be smug and condescending. Jake would follow Holden's lead, talking down to his troubled little sister. Ty and Marcus might be the best of the bunch to approach, but even they would scold Eve and make her feel worse than she already did. And Tim…

Oh, Tim.

As Eve stared out the tiny window into a courtyard with neglected landscaping, she decided she had no choice but to play nice with Saul and give him whatever he wanted. None of this made sense. But it didn't have to. Eve told herself she would cope by taking it one hour at a time. One minute at a time, if necessary. Just like her therapist had taught her. She'd use what she did have at her disposal: her sex appeal.

The thought caused Eve to instinctively place a protective hand over her lower abdomen.

The baby.

She had nearly forgotten about the baby. No one knew about the baby yet. Eve herself didn't even know if the baby was real. Not for sure.

Acting on impulse, Eve had purchased an early result pregnancy test at the San Francisco airport. It had been seven days since she and Tim first made love during what Eve had thought was this month's ovulation window. Figuring it was worth a shot, she had peed on the test stick in a shiny, silver stall in the airport bathroom as harried travelers whizzed in and out around her, their rolling suitcases clanking against the hard floor.

Tim doesn't know. I need to tell him.

Eve felt another wave of panic threaten to overwhelm her as she moved around Saul's bathroom. Frantically, she dumped the contents of her purse out in the pedestal sink as she searched for her phone one more time.

I need to tell Tim. It can't wait. He has to know about the baby.

Unable to find her phone and scared of losing her mind again, Eve leaned back against the glass shower door as she tried to calm herself. Remembering what her therapist had said about talking things through when she felt herself getting upset, Eve decided to improvise.

She turned the shower on as hot as she could stand, then she took off her clothes and stepped inside. Using the handheld shower head, she placed it against her ear like a telephone receiver.

"Tim? It's me, Eve. *Your* Eve. I know… You've probably been worried about me. But I'm here. I'm okay."

She whispered so only Tim could hear, the noise of the water masking her one-sided conversation.

"I have something important to tell you, my love. I took one of those instant pregnancy tests in the airport yesterday. And, Tim… There was a line for a positive result! It was a faint line, but it was there. I know it was. We're having a baby!"

Tears came again as she talked, even more softly now.

"I can't wait, Tim. If it's a little girl, we could name her Isla. Get it? Because she was conceived in Islamorada? I think it's the perfect choice. And if it's a boy, well, we should name him after you. Timothy Fischer II. I've never known a better man."

Eve placed her free hand against her heart. She had waited so long to be pregnant with Tim's baby. She couldn't understand why all of this other bad stuff was happening at the same time.

It wasn't fair.

"But Tim, I've gotten myself into some trouble," Eve continued, still speaking into the shower head. "I'm sorry. I can't get back home to you right away. I lost some of my stuff. I'm not sure where… It doesn't matter. But I'm with a nice man right now, and I think I have to play along so he'll keep being kind to me. I wanted you to come get me. You didn't…"

Eve looked up at the smooth ceiling, sky blue paint beginning to chip around the edges. She took a series of deep breaths to steady herself.

"I love you, Tim," she said. "Remember that. Always."

Then she returned the shower head to its mounting bracket above her head. She turned off the water without washing her body or her hair, despite the presence of an easily accessible bottle of shampoo and a bar of soap.

She got dressed again in her dirty clothes, ready to face Saul and to give him whatever he wanted.

9

"I've got something," Jake said to the others as he bounded into the living room.

They'd been searching for hours, painstakingly combing through Eve and Tim's belongings. They were growing weary, and anxious.

"Good man," Wilder said to his son, patting him enthusiastically on the back. "What have you got?"

"I was able to access the voicemail box on their home telephone line," Jake explained.

"Wow," Wilder replied. "I'm surprised they still use a home phone."

"Yeah, I'm glad they do, because there's a message there from a man at the Islamorada hotel where they stayed," Jake continued. "He said they have Eve's mobile phone."

"What a catch," Marcus said. "That's a big lead."

"Right on," Holden added, motioning with a thumbs up. "Good job, Jake."

"Where did they find it?" Phoebe asked. "And when?"

"The voicemail said another guest turned the phone in after finding it in the sand, out by one of the cabanas. I got the idea they don't know how long it had been lost. Meaning, they're not sure how long it was out there."

Jake had a tendency to restate the same idea more than once when he spoke.

"I wonder if the thing still works," Wilder mused.

"I remember Eve mentioning that the hotel they were going to stay at had a private beach," Phoebe added. "I believe it was a locally-owned resort. On the Atlantic side. Jake, do you know the name of the place?"

"No, but this guy… He said his name is Roger Wilson. He left a phone number."

"Call him!" Phoebe said.

"I'll do it right now," Jake confirmed.

Less than a minute later, Phoebe's phone dinged. It was Monique. She had received Phoebe's Facebook message and was writing back with her phone number. She was willing to help. Monique's cooperation was a major break, because Phoebe had already tried calling both the San Francisco airport and the airline. Citing privacy concerns, neither would tell her whether Eve and Tim had been on their scheduled flight.

"Hang in there, everyone," Wilder urged. "We will keep working on this issue, and we will see it through. We will find them. I know we will."

Jake went into his sister's office to make his call while Phoebe made hers in the living room. The others gathered around, moving back-and-forth between the two rooms, eager to hear any scrap of information that would help them find Eve.

They all knew that the longer Eve was missing, the worse the trouble she was likely in. They also knew that darkness came early this time of year. They wanted to locate Eve during daylight hours if at all possible.

Holden stepped close to his dad while he waited for the phone conversations to take place. "What do you make of these new developments?"

Wilder widened his stance, standing with his feet more than shoulder width apart. He stared straight ahead at nothing in particular as he tousled the hair on the back of his head.

"I don't know, son," Wilder replied. "I guess I'm cautiously optimistic about Eve's phone being found. Maybe that's why she hasn't been in touch. Maybe whatever is going on is no big deal at all, and it just seems like it is because of the lost phone."

"Do you really believe that?" Holden asked.

Wilder shook his head, his body giving him away before his words did. "I don't know. I want to. I'm pretty shaken up, truth be told."

"I can see that," Holden confirmed. "I hope this isn't too much…"

Unbeknownst to most of the family, Wilder was dealing with a heart condition. Phoebe and Holden were the only ones he had told. He didn't want to alarm anyone until he knew more about what was happening. All they knew so far was that Wilder's heart would race so fast that doctors had to shock it to bring it back to a normal rhythm.

A number of options were on the table, including medication and surgery. Wilder was a man who didn't like to inconvenience people, especially not his beloved family. He had made Phoebe and Wilder promise to stay tight-lipped until the doctors made a definitive diagnosis.

"Nonsense," Wilder said. "Don't even think it. This is my daughter we're talking about. And my son-in-law. My sole concern right now is making sure they're safe."

"Okay," Holden replied. "But take care of yourself, Dad. The last thing we want is something happening to you as a result of all this stress. Eve would never forgive herself."

"I hear you, son," Wilder replied.

"Hear you about what?" Ty asked as he joined his dad and brother. "What are you guys talking about?"

Wilder shot Holden a warning look.

Luckily, Holden was good at thinking on his feet. He was also good at telling partial truths so as not to be caught in a lie. Not technically.

"We were just talking about how stressful this whole thing is," Holden explained. "I don't know about you, Jake, but I'm on edge. I'm seriously concerned for Sis right now. You know how she gets."

"Yeah, I do," Ty confirmed. "I've been thinking about it myself. I wonder if we relied too heavily on Tim."

"That's a possibility," Wilder agreed.

"Think about it," Ty continued. "With us watching out for Eve, we can divide the responsibility up amongst ourselves so that no one person has too much to bear."

Holden nodded and continued his brother's thought. "But for Tim, we've let the weight of that responsibility fall squarely on his shoulders. Damn. You're right, Ty. We may have dropped the ball on that one."

The three men looked at each other. No one wanted to say what they were all thinking.

"Do you suspect this will be as bad as last time?" Ty asked. He looked to his big brother and their father for reassurance.

Wilder hung his head and stared at the floor, content to let Holden answer for the time being. The two of them were in a strange place in life. Wilder was the head of the family and still capable, but Holden was doing such a good job as leader that the elder Blackburn found himself gradually relinquishing his role to the next generation.

"I don't know, Ty," Holden explained. "I'm not trying to be cagey. I truly don't know. What happened before was a long time ago. Before Eve got connected with the professionals who helped stabilize her. I'd like to think that was all in the past and that this time is nothing more than a misunderstanding."

"Yeah," Ty agreed. "Wouldn't that be nice?"

Holden echoed his sentiment. "I'd like to see Eve and Tim walk through that front door. I wouldn't even care if they were mad as hell at us for rooting through their things."

Wilder chuckled. "Right," he added. "Let them be mad. I'd take it."

"And if they can't walk through that door for some reason," Holden continued. "I'd like them to call us. Text us. Facebook message us. Anything."

Ty and Wilder nodded their agreement.

"We just don't know," Wilder said solemnly.

As the men stood, staring, Jake finished his phone call and returned to join them.

"What's up?" Holden asked. "What did Roger from Islamorada have to say?"

"Unfortunately," Jake replied. "Not much. He offered to mail Eve's phone back to her home address since it was already on record, but he insisted that he couldn't share any additional information unless it was requested by law enforcement."

"Let me guess," Phoebe said, entering from the next room. "Privacy concerns?"

"Exactly."

"What about you, Mom?" Holden inquired. "Anything useful from Monique?"

Phoebe took a long, deep breath before answering.

"Yes," she confirmed. "But it isn't exactly the news we were hoping to hear."

"Okay," Wilder said. "Get on with it then. What?"

Phoebe winced as she talked, closing her eyes tightly.

"Monique checked the passenger records for me. Eve was on the plane. She arrived in San Francisco yesterday afternoon, as scheduled."

"Good," Holden replied. "At least we know that much. Our girl made it back to California where we can get to her."

Wilder could tell that his wife was holding back. "There's more," he said, raising a hand up to stop his son.

"That's right," Phoebe confirmed. "Eve was on the flight. Tim was not. In fact, Monique can't find any record of him boarding a plane since they arrived in Miami. He didn't make a return trip."

10

Phoebe leaned on a wall to prop herself up as she and her family reeled from the revelation. Things were officially out of control. Dangerously so. Her daughter may have been an adult, but she wasn't capable of taking care of herself like most adults.

Phoebe and Wilder never would have let her go all the way to Florida if Tim hadn't been with her. True, it was a lot to ask of Tim. But he had signed up for it. He chose Eve, and when he married her, he knew the responsibility he was taking on. He loved her despite her disease.

"Mom," Holden said gently, his eyes full of worry. "It's time to call the police."

Phoebe shrugged her shoulders and pressed harder against the wall, as if it would keep her upright. "I don't know," she said.

Wilder walked over and placed his arms around his wife, scooping her into him. Holden placed a hand on his mom's shoulder as her tears fell. Feeling the collective hurt, Jake, Ty, and Marcus joined in, each placing a hand on Phoebe's back.

"Mom?" Holden tried again.

The officers and detectives on the Rosemary Run police force were some of the best anywhere. They were thorough, kind, and responsive. Holden knew a few of them from school. And several kept a watchful eye on Brambleberry Fields, even providing help with traffic management during large events.

"I know," Phoebe said. "I know."

"Holden," Wilder said, leaning his chin on his wife's shoulder as he held her. "Make the call, please. Start with Officer James Tatum. If he's on duty today, ask him to join us here for a preliminary discussion."

Holden nodded, then scurried to the next room to get it done.

"It's okay," Wilder said to his wife. "Whatever we're facing, we'll do it together."

"I know," Phoebe repeated. "But I can feel the dread in the pit of my stomach. This is bad."

The group agreed. And they believed her. They trusted Phoebe's instincts.

It was less than twenty minutes from the time Holden made the call until Officer Tatum showed up at Eve and Tim's front door. He looked somber as he stepped inside the house and sat down on the floral-print sofa amongst the Blackburn family, his uniform crisp and firm. Although they weren't close friends, James knew the Blackburns well enough to have been made aware of Eve's specific vulnerabilities.

"Thank you for coming," Holden said. "We appreciate how fast you got over here."

"I'm happy to help," James replied. "It's good to see you folks. I just wish it were under better circumstances."

Everyone nodded, too upset to spend much time on small talk.

"Let's get right to the heart of the matter, then," Holden prompted.

"Yes," James agreed. "What's going on?"

"Like I mentioned on the phone," Holden began. "It's Eve. And her husband Tim Fischer."

"Okay. I don't know Tim, but I remember Eve. She has that pretty red hair like my wife, Rebecca."

Phoebe smiled. "That's right. Gorgeous red hair. Both of them."

Holden continued. "Sis— I mean, Eve— and Tim went away nine days ago for a vacation in the Florida Keys. Islamorada. Although, they moved between the Keys and Miami, so their activities were not confined to Islamorada. But that's where the resort they stayed at is located..."

"Got it," James replied, listening closely and jotting down notes on a small pad taken from his breast pocket. "Do you know the name of the resort?"

Everyone looked at Jake, hoping he got the name when he spoke with Roger.

"Yes," Jake inserted, referencing a note on his smartphone. "Keys Cove Resort and Marina. It's a local place. Not affiliated with a larger hospitality company."

"And you've spoken with them, I assume?"

"We have," Jake confirmed. "Another guest found

Eve's phone in the sand on their private beach a few days ago. They have it at the front desk and can mail it here to her home address. But they won't tell me anything else. Not without an inquiry from law enforcement."

"Right," James said. "Go on."

James gestured toward Holden to continue, furrowing his brow as he moved. James was thinking, and the Blackburns appreciated his sharp focus.

"They were supposed to return home yesterday. They had a flight into San Francisco, arriving yesterday afternoon," Holden explained. "Mom— Phoebe— has a friend who works at SFO. She looked into it and found that Eve arrived home on that flight, but Tim didn't. And, well, Eve isn't likely to do well without Tim."

"And Tim isn't likely to leave her," Phoebe added. "Something is wrong."

James pursed his lips. "I assume you've tried to contact them."

"Yes," Holden confirmed. "But Eve lost her phone. We don't know what's happening with Tim's. His goes right to voicemail. And he didn't show up for work today."

James raised his eyebrows.

Wilder jumped in. "Eve's phone is still on our family plan with the cell phone company, but Tim's is not. We can't get any info on his location or call records."

"Does he have family around? Anyone he keeps in close touch with besides you folks?" James asked.

"No," Wilder replied. "That's the thing. We called Tim's mom in Phoenix. She hasn't heard from him since he phoned to wish her a Merry Christmas."

"And I assume Tim isn't the type to skip out on work without calling?"

"Never," Wilder confirmed. "The guy has a PhD. He's serious about his work. Environmental sciences. And he's diligent."

"Okay," James said as he continued to scribble furiously. "And no one has seen either of them here in Rosemary Run yesterday or today?"

"Not as far as we know," Holden answered. "Eve's friend, Victoria Baker, alerted me to unusual postings on social media. That's how we knew Eve hadn't returned home as scheduled."

"Oh?" James asked. "I'd like you to show those social media accounts to me. And give me all the names and phone numbers for people you've spoken to. My colleagues and I will probably want to contact each of these individuals and take formal statements. Also, I'll need descriptions of height, weight, age, and any identifying marks such as tattoos or birthmarks. I'll need to know everything you do about what they were last seen wearing and who they were seen with."

"Understood," Holden replied.

"To confirm, you entered this home with a key?" James asked.

The Blackburns looked at each other. They didn't want to lie to a police officer, that was for sure. But they also didn't want to lose access to the house. There might be more clues lurking within it that could help them find Eve.

Holden spoke up, comfortable with his half-truths in this particular situation. "That's right. I entered with a key." He didn't mention Mona, or the fact that Eve and Tim hadn't personally given any of them a key.

"Okay," James confirmed. "Got it. Let me get this info back to the station and we'll look into a few things. I should have something to report by evening."

Phoebe bristled. She didn't like the idea of waiting until evening, even though it was now only a few hours away.

Holden spoke, verbalizing what they were all thinking. "James, forgive me. But what does that mean, exactly?" he asked.

"Which part?" the officer returned.

"All of it. Will Eve be considered a missing person? Will Tim? Will there be an investigation? Please... break it down for us."

James shifted his weight backward, placing one hand on his belt near his radio. As if on cue, the radio crackled, then blurted the voice of a female dispatcher. James turned the small dial to lower the volume. "That's hard to say. Eve and Tim are adults. And neither is mentally nor physically impaired, or elderly. In general, missing persons reports are filed for an adult when an individual may need medical, legal, or other help. We'll first need to determine that Tim and Eve are, in fact, missing. Maybe they decided to extend their trip, or to take a detour. Maybe Tim took a bus back. Who knows? There are dozens of possibilities."

Phoebe sat up straight in her chair. "But Eve *is* mentally impaired."

James smiled his reassurance, choosing his words carefully. "Mrs. Blackburn..."

"Please, call me Phoebe."

"Okay, Phoebe," James continued. "I've heard rumors about Eve's troubles. I think most Rosemary Run residents have, after the incident that happened when she was a teenager. But we'll need more than rumors to take action here. Does Eve have a diagnosis that confirms mental impairment?"

"She does," Phoebe said, her voice cracking.

Eve's diagnosis was one that the Blackburn clan avoided discussing. Especially Phoebe. No amount of business success or accolades at Brambleberry Fields made up for what the matriarch felt was a critical, personal failing, so she didn't want to talk about it. Phoebe considered her daughter defective. In a big way.

Wilder placed his hand over his wife's while Holden took a deep breath, at the ready.

Phoebe spoke before either of them had to.

"She's… Eve is…"

"It's okay, Mom," Holden urged.

"She's bipolar," Phoebe confessed, sputtering. "Bipolar I, the most severe form of the illness… with manic episodes. And she's been trying to conceive, so I suspect that she hasn't been taking her medication."

11

Saul was sitting at his two-seater kitchen table when Eve returned from the shower. He smoked a cigarette while tracing the lines of the linoleum top with his fingers.

His place was simple but orderly. Eve thought it a typical bachelor pad. For a lower-income bachelor, anyway. It lacked the sophisticated decor and comforts of the beautiful house Tim had bought them on Crickett Lane.

"You okay?" Saul asked, blowing smoke to one side.

"I'm good," Eve replied. "Really good."

She put one hand on her hip and raised the opposite knee, trying to be seductive.

"That's good to hear," Saul said. "I'm still worried about you. Are you sure you don't want me to call anyone?"

"That's sweet," Eve returned. "But I seem to have misplaced my cell phone."

Saul stood up quickly. "Here, you can use mine," he offered.

"That's okay," she said. "Maybe later. I don't…"

He looked at her, puzzled.

"I don't have anyone to call. That's all."

"Okay," he said. "I could take you somewhere. How does that sound?"

"No, thanks," Eve said. "I have other plans for you today."

Saul smiled. He didn't know what to make of Eve, but he thought she was very beautiful. He wanted to spend more time with her. "You do?"

"That's right. I do," she confirmed, unbuttoning the top three buttons of her shirt to expose her ample cleavage. "Like… Fun things."

Eve let her purse fall to the floor, then she broke into an impromptu dance. Twirling, leaping, and sashaying as she stripped her clothes off, she put her body on full display for Saul. She didn't need music. Instead, Eve hummed a sultry tune as she went.

The dance made her feel sexy. Her sex drive had been on high lately. She needed it like a junkie needed a fix. This situation with Saul was a way to meet that need. So, what if getting a sexual fix had the added bonus of passing the time and keeping Eve away from the critical eyes of her family?

One day, one hour, and one moment at a time. For this moment, she wanted Saul. She wanted to feel him inside of her again.

"Look at you," he said. "You're a dancer."

Eve shuffled over to where Saul was sitting and

plopped down on his lap. She didn't seem aware that she was still dirty, and beginning to stink. Saul leaned into her, then moved his head back, reacting to the stench. Dried blood, greasy hair, morning hangover breath, and body odor were not a good combination.

"Did you take a shower?" he asked. "I thought I heard the water running."

"I did."

"Um… Did you find the soap?" He seemed reluctant to ask. "I can get some toothpaste. Whatever you need."

"I'm clean…" Eve said, practically chirping she was talking so fast. "Come, Saul Milton, dance with me." She leaped up again, parading around the room at top speed now.

"Oh… okay, okay," he replied, joining her.

Saul put his cigarette out into a large silver ashtray that looked like it belonged in an entirely different house. It was posh. Elegant, even. Eve thought that maybe it had been a gift. Although she scarcely noticed the details of her surroundings on this particular day, the silver ashtray stood out.

As the butt smoldered in the background, sheltered by the elegant silver, Eve took Saul by the hand and led him in a waltz, then a slow dance. She continued to hum, switching tunes to match the dance. She moved faster and faster, in what seemed to Saul like a dizzying pace. Eve didn't appear affected. Something was driving her. She had superhuman energy.

"Listen," Saul began as he slowed to a stop in the middle of the floor. "Don't be offended by this, please…"

"Uh huh?" Eve said quickly.

"Did you take something?"

"What do you mean?" she asked, her eyes flicking towards his and then quickly away. "Are you asking if I stole something out of your bathroom? I'm not a thief, Saul."

"I mean, are you high right now?"

Eve's face balled up. "No. No! Why would you ask me that?"

"I just…"

"No, no, no," she continued, growing angry. "I don't take drugs unless they're prescribed by my doctor. No, sir... What kind of girl do you take me for?"

She leaned her head back dramatically and let out a loud cackle. Her mood seemed to change minute to minute.

"I'm not saying there's anything wrong with it," Saul replied, clarifying his position. "In fact, I have some... *recreational* substances we could partake in. If you aren't scared. But I thought maybe you had gotten the party started without me… All that energy and… Earlier..."

Eve continued moving and flailing around the room while humming, like a wounded songbird trying to take flight. It was pitiful, really. But Saul didn't know what he was witnessing. His only frame of reference for someone acting like Eve was drug related. He thought she had done this to herself. He thought she had sought this mania.

"Kiss me," Eve said suddenly, grabbing Saul around the neck and pulling his lips to hers. He pulled back, her hygiene a concern. But she persisted, pulling him closer and wrapping one leg around his.

He narrowed his eyes, considering the situation.

"Hey, how did it get dark already?" Eve asked, her attention shifting outdoors. "The sun was out and now it's gone. Poof!"

"Yeah, that's what happens at night," Saul said.

Eve began to laugh hysterically, pulling on Saul as she flailed. "That's hilarious!"

"What?"

"What you said," she explained through laughter. "That… What you… That it gets dark every night. *Of course*, it does. You're funny, Saul. The way you said it was… funny."

She careened, one hand around his neck. She used her free hand to caress his groin, awakening it with her touch. He stiffened. "Okay, screw it. Let's party," Saul said.

"Yay!" Eve cheered. "What will we have at our party? A house party. It will be the best house party ever…"

"If you say so, yeah," Saul agreed. "I'll get us a drink to start, then maybe we'll add something else to the mix. We'll see where the night takes us. You like whiskey?"

"Sure do."

"Wait here," Saul said, his face more animated than it had been all day. "This will be fun."

It wasn't long until both Saul and Eve were heavily intoxicated, pawing at each other and enjoying an array of sex acts and positions.

All without protection.

Then Saul brought out a syringe and a needle and asked Eve if she wanted to try injecting heroin.

12

I t was nearly eight o'clock by the time James got back in touch with the Blackburns to report on his preliminary findings.

Phoebe, Wilder, Holden, Jake, Ty, and Marcus had all stayed at Eve and Tim's house. They were unsure of what to do with themselves. No one wanted to miss an important update or a chance to be helpful. When Holden brought his wife up to speed, Lorelei had shown up with burgers for everyone. They did little more than pick at them, though, their stomachs too upset to eat.

Victoria had joined the group after Holden updated her on the deepening level of concern for her friend. She sat alone on an armchair, twirling her dark curly hair around and around one finger. Her brown skin looked pale. She was sick about all of this. Just like the rest of the bunch.

"James, come in," Holden said from the porch as the officer got out of his squad car and shut the door. Holden was eager to hear an update.

"Hey, Holden," James said casually. He was dropping formality as much as possible to put the family at ease. "How are you holding up?"

"We've been better," Holden replied as James stepped into the house and smiled somberly at the others. "I hope you have some good news for us. We could sure use it right about now."

James sat down in the middle of the sofa, the same spot he had occupied earlier in the afternoon. He looked tired.

"I can only imagine what you're going through," James said.

"I know," Holden replied. "I'm sure you're probably home with your wife by this time of evening on most nights. We appreciate you working late for us."

"It's no problem. Really."

There was an uneasiness in the air. Everyone involved wanted to get on with it and learn what James knew. But at the same time, they didn't. They figured the news wasn't good. Wishing to remain oblivious— or maybe, in denial— a while longer was a powerful motivator. They wanted to hang onto it a few minutes more.

"I guess we should go ahead," Holden said reluctantly.

"Yes, certainly," James replied.

Wilder inserted himself, speaking up. "Tell us what you know, Officer Tatum."

James cleared his throat. He had delivered tough news hundreds of times, but it never got any easier. Especially with people he knew and liked. It was one of the drawbacks of being a police officer in a small town.

"So," James began. "First of all, you folks are right. Eve and Tim are missing. We have enough evidence to have determined that. I've filed a missing persons report on both of them."

Phoebe rocked gently in her seat, a hand over her mouth. It was becoming a familiar stance. She didn't speak. Victoria adopted a similar pose. Something about a hand over the mouth seemed to help the ladies steady themselves. Maybe it was self-soothing, like babies do when they suck on their fingers.

"Good," Wilder said. "That will move things along. It's good… Under the circumstances."

James nodded. "It's an important step. Now, we're investigating."

"Go on," Holden said.

"Let's start with Tim," James confirmed. "I followed up with Roger at the Islamorada resort. He told me a few pieces of interesting information related to Tim's activity during the time he and Eve were guests."

"Okay," Wilder said.

"Roger reports that Tim was last seen on the property on Thursday. That's three days before he and Eve were scheduled to check out."

"What?" Ty asked, baffled.

"Roger says Eve checked out alone yesterday morning. He had his manager review the security cameras to confirm. No sign of Tim since Thursday."

"What do you make of that?" Holden asked. "Do you think they had an argument and split up for some reason? I ask to cover the bases, but that doesn't sound like Tim.

Even though Eve's moods can be rocky, their relationship is harmonious."

James nodded. "I figured you'd say that. I'm not sure what to think yet, because anything is possible."

"What else do you have on Tim?" Wilder asked.

"Not much. And therein lies the story. It's why I'm concerned. We talked to Tim's boss and some of his colleagues. We also contacted his mom. By all accounts, Tim isn't the type of guy to disappear into thin air."

"Yeah," Wilder mused.

"We also contacted the wireless carrier that serves Tim's mobile phone."

"Oh?" Holden asked. "Did they tell you anything useful?"

"They did. Tim's phone hasn't been used since Thursday. It was still transmitting from the resort up until Friday afternoon, which is probably when the battery ran out. Once a phone powers off, it can't be tracked."

"Damn," Wilder said softly. "James, what do we do then? If Tim has disappeared, how in the world will we find him? And… I don't mean that we care any less about Tim… But… Eve?"

"I understand," James replied. "Eve's your child. And she's… more vulnerable."

"Yes."

"We're sick about it all," Phoebe mumbled. "We want them both back."

"As for Eve," James continued. "We know she checked out of the resort in the Keys yesterday afternoon and that she used a ride sharing service to get to the airport in Miami. Like your friend Monique told you, Eve made it onto her flight and arrived safely in San Francisco. But I'm afraid that's where our certainty ends. No one has seen her since, as far as we know."

"And she hasn't used her phone, correct?" Victoria asked, kicking one foot nervously as she talked.

"Right," James confirmed. "Not since days ago in Islamorada. I asked Roger to overnight her phone to the station. Our tech and forensics guys will get their hands on it as soon as we receive the device tomorrow. And I have Roger's team searching for Tim's phone. Hopefully, they'll find and send it, too."

"How about bank records?" Holden asked. "We haven't accessed any of those from our end yet. I'm not sure we can."

"Already done," James confirmed. "We checked their bank and credit card accounts. No activity from Tim's since Thursday morning."

"And Eve's?" Phoebe asked expectantly. She looked almost hopeful, like she hadn't thought that far.

"She used her ATM card to pull out five hundred dollars in cash at the Miami airport yesterday morning. She hasn't used any of her accounts since."

Wilder shook his head hard. "So they've both just… vanished?"

"I know it seems that way," James said. "But people don't just disappear. There are answers out there. It's our job to find those answers, and to find Tim and Eve."

Tensions were rising in the group. The Blackburns were becoming restless. Agitated. They didn't know what to ask. They didn't know what to do with themselves.

"So, what happens next?" Holden asked, speaking for the group.

"Good question," James confirmed. "I want you folks to have access to as much information as possible. The case is being handled by two of our best investigators: Neil Fredericks and Luke Hemming. They're already working. They'll be consulting with the Monroe County Sheriff's Office in the Florida Keys, as well as the Miami-Dade Police Department and the San Francisco Police Department as needed."

"Good," Wilder said. "I know both men. They're excellent investigators. What can *we* do?"

"I know you want to do something to help," James continued. "I get that. But it's best if you let us handle things now. Besides, I know you folks have a resort to run. And I don't know if you've heard, but forecasters are saying we're going to get snow tomorrow night. It may make a real mess for business around here if the highway shuts down."

"We heard," Holden confirmed. "Our employees know about the storm and are working to prepare."

"But frankly," Wilder said, jumping in. "Nothing at the resort matters right now. We need to find them. Eve…"

James leaned back, thoughtful. He rested his hand on his belt like he had earlier. "Look, family members often bungle police investigations and cause more harm than they do good, but I realize this situation with Eve is… different."

"Yes?" Phoebe asked, hopeful again.

"I'd like you folks to come in and meet the detectives right away. We'll take formal statements from each of you.

Once that's done, if you want to conduct your own search for Eve and Tim… Go ahead. Just keep us informed. I want you to let us know if you find anything at all that might be helpful. Understood?"

"Yes!" the group said in unison.

"Thank you," Holden said to James, leaning forward and slapping him enthusiastically on the knee. "It feels better to do something. Anything…"

"I really do get it," James replied. "When my brother-in-law died suddenly, I couldn't just sit on my hands and wait."

Phoebe let out an audible moan at the mention of death.

"I'm sorry, Phoebe," James said. "I didn't mean to imply… I was…"

"It's okay," Wilder said. "We know you're trying to comfort us, James. We're just a little jumpy right now. Truly, it's okay."

Phoebe closed her eyes, leaning in to her husband.

James nodded, hesitant to say another word.

"Thank you, James," Holden affirmed. "We'll follow you to the station."

"I'll wait here," Ty said. "You know… In case they come home. One of you come switch with me when you're done giving your statement."

James walked to Ty and put his hand on the younger man's shoulder. "We've got this. The Rosemary Run Police Department is here for you. An officer will be here around the clock in case they come home. Be with your family, Ty. You need each other right now."

Wiping tears, the Blackburns nodded their agreement

and appreciation. They piled into their vehicles along with Victoria, then followed James' squad car to the police station downtown, tail lights gleaming against the darkness.

Although no one said it out loud, the procession reminded them of a funeral. They silently prayed to everything holy that they wouldn't be attending a funeral for Eve or Tim anytime soon.

13

The police station was bustling when the Blackburns arrived. Its position on a hill overlooking the valley gave it an air of authority. Inside, lamps shone on crisp brown file folders as officers scribbled notes, and phones rang urgently. It looked like every desk and station was occupied.

It wasn't often that one of Rosemary Run's own went missing. The fact that a husband and wife were both missing made those on the force even more eager to get to the bottom of what had happened and bring them home safe. Not to mention, Eve's particular vulnerabilities warranted extra attention.

"Mr. and Mrs. Blackburn," Neil Fredericks began as he reached a hand out to shake theirs. He had been waiting at the front of the building to greet them. "I'm sorry we're seeing each other under these circumstances, but I want you to know you're in good hands. My team and I are going to do everything possible to find Eve and Tim."

"Thank you, Neil," Wilder said as he shook the investigator's hand. "Like I said to James a while ago, I'm sure you're usually home with your family by this time of night."

"Usually," Neil replied. "But Cate and the kids don't mind. They'd rather I was here helping find your kiddo." He leaned forward and lowered his voice. "We all know they're our babies, no matter how old they get."

Phoebe smiled. It was her first smile in hours. "You're a good one," she said softly to Neil.

"I second that," Wilder added. "We appreciate you being here."

Neil introduced himself to the others, shaking hands and offering words of comfort. When everyone was familiar, he led them back to a conference room where they could meet his partner, Luke Hemming. Officers stopped what they were doing to bow their heads and show their respect as the Blackburns walked past. It was a small kindness. One that was greatly appreciated. Although the treatment they received made the family realize just how serious Eve and Tim's situation was. It was sobering.

"Hello, folks," Luke said as they shuffled into the conference room.

The room was stark and unattractive, a far cry from the posh, glass-walled conference room at Brambleberry Fields.

A heavy set Asian lady wearing a tight-fitting uniform stuck her head in the door. "Margaret Fischer is on her way from Phoenix," she announced, glancing at her smartwatch. "Her flight is scheduled to arrive at our local airfield around eleven o'clock tonight." The woman's name tag read Officer Woo.

"Thank you, Pamela," Luke replied. "Keep me posted."

It was nice that Luke used the woman's first name. Every little thing that felt informal was welcome, as far as the Blackburns were concerned.

"One of us can pick Margaret up when she arrives," Holden offered. "We met her at Eve and Tim's wedding."

"If you'd like," Luke said. "I'll leave that up to you."

"She and Tim aren't close from what I understand," Holden continued. "But it's the right thing to do. She's still family. She must be distraught over all of this. I know I would be. Hell, I *am*."

"I agree," Wilder said. "Margaret's husband died years ago, and she never remarried. I imagine it would be especially difficult to face a situation like this alone. We'll take care of her as best we can."

Wilder looked at his sons as he spoke, a directive. They received the message loud and clear. Then Wilder took his wife's hand and gave it a squeeze. Phoebe had been uncharacteristically quiet for hours now. Wilder was beginning to worry about her.

"Good," Luke confirmed. "We've got some time until Margaret arrives. We'll try to get your statements and get you out of here by then."

It felt strange to the Blackburns to think about getting out of the police station. Where would they go? What would they do with themselves? James had said they could help search for Eve and Tim, but they weren't sure how.

Holden intended to take the lead to make it easier on

his parents. Even though he wasn't sure yet how he would do so. He hoped the right words would come to him when it was time. He stared at the stains on the old hardwood planks on the station's floor as he thought about his responsibility to the others. He knew full well that being a leader meant more than taking credit when things were going well. He knew it was even more important that he came through for them now, when they needed him most. He also knew that he had to protect his dad's secret and his fragile heart. The burden weighed heavily on him.

Neil closed the door to the room and smiled sympathetically. "Can I get you folks anything to drink? Or to eat?"

"We can't eat," Phoebe mumbled.

"My wife brought us some burgers a while ago," Holden added. "But we couldn't get much down."

"I understand," Neil replied. "But it's important that you keep your strength up. This is a marathon, not a sprint."

They looked at each other, reluctantly agreeing.

"Do it for Eve and Tim?" Neil tried. "How about I get some pasta dishes ordered in? Nothing too spicy. Maybe some grilled chicken on top? Pasta noodles should be bland enough to go down easy and settle your stomachs. Not to get all technical on you, but I'm a nutrition junkie and have studied up on this. Carbs like pasta actually help to increase serotonin, and in this case, may help you cope with what you're facing. And you need the energy."

"Okay, okay," Phoebe replied, taking her credit card out of her purse. "Use my card. Pasta for the room. We'll eat together. Order from that noodle place on Sixth Street if they'll still deliver this time of night."

"Done," Neil said, winking to thank her then scurrying out to place the order. "I know that place. It's near my house. I'll send someone for pickup if they won't deliver."

"You guys sure are taking good care of us," Wilder said to Luke once the door closed behind Neil. "I hope that doesn't mean anything we should be alarmed about..."

Luke sighed heavily and pursed his large, pink lips. He leaned forward over the table and laced his fingers together in front of him. "The situation is worrisome, I won't make light of that. Let us be as good as we can to you. Consider it a perk of living in a small town."

Wilder nodded. "I hear you." He shot a knowing glance at his wife as he spoke. The two of them knew the stakes. They were trying to hold it together for their kids, but they were terrified.

"We just can't thank you enough," Holden added. "You guys are the best."

"We do what we can," Luke replied. "Now, I want to go over a few things before we take your statements."

The group nodded, eager to get the process started.

"First of all," Luke continued. "None of you are suspects. We don't think you've done anything to harm Eve or Tim. But there are protocols we are required to follow. Part of that will include asking each of you about the last time you saw or talked to them, your whereabouts the last few days, and other questions that might be uncomfortable. Try not to take it too personally."

"We understand," Holden said.

Luke's face was serious as he spoke. "We never know when what may have seemed like a minor detail will be the clue that helps us find them. We have to be thorough." He felt bad to put the family through any more trauma. But it had to be done.

"Okay," Phoebe said. "But I can tell you right now, we didn't have anything to do with this. Our failure is not watching over Eve more closely... We thought..." She broke into tears and got too choked up to finish.

Holden was sitting beside his mom. He reached out a hand and placed it on her outstretched forearm. "We thought Tim would watch over her," he said, finishing his mom's sentence.

"Let's talk about Eve's condition for a minute," Luke prompted. "I understand she's been diagnosed as bipolar I?"

"That's right," Holden replied.

"Is she medicated? Officer Tatum mentioned something about her possibly being off her medication?"

"Yes," Holden confirmed. "We know that she and Tim were trying to conceive. So, Mom thinks maybe she stopped taking her medicine for that reason."

"I can feel it," Phoebe said. "And besides, I can't imagine this situation happening otherwise. She... has a history."

Luke thumbed through the folder placed nearby on the table, looking at Eve's record. "I see here that she had a brush with authorities when she was a teenager. That was before I arrived in Rosemary Run from Reno. Do you mind telling me about that? I'd rather hear it from you."

Holden, Wilder, and Phoebe looked at each other

sheepishly, then at the rest of the group. They had tried for so long to keep what happened under wraps. It was embarrassing for the whole family. They didn't want the family's good reputation around town blemished. Most of all, they didn't want Eve labeled as crazy. Bipolar disorder was misunderstood as it was. The Blackburns didn't want Eve to carry a stigma that might keep her from making friends, holding jobs, and more. She was theirs. They wanted to protect her.

"I'll tell it," Holden offered, ever the good son, willing to take a stand for the family.

Wilder raised a hand to stop him. "It's not your responsibility, son. I'll tell the story. She's my daughter."

Luke smiled at Wilder, impressed by his fathering. "Go ahead."

Wilder took a deep breath, fidgeting in his seat.

"It's okay," Luke said softly. "We're all friends here, Wilder. People who are mentally or physically impaired or in need of medical attention are in more danger the longer they are missing. It sounds like Eve needs us badly. We want to understand what she is dealing with so we can get her home safe."

"I know," Wilder said. "It's just… hard… But you're exactly right. It's important that you know everything so you can find our girl."

"And Tim," Holden added.

"Yes, and Tim." Wilder jerked his neck to one side, then cracked his knuckles as he prepared to open up. "Okay, so... When our daughter was a teenager, symptoms of her disease were hard for us to recognize. She was really irritable. I mean, *really* irritable. And she had mood swings that were scary bad. Extreme sadness would sideline her for days at a time. She'd miss school. And we felt her slipping away from us. We'd only had boys until Eve, so we thought maybe it was just teenage girl hormones."

"But it wasn't?" Luke asked, listening closely.

"Unfortunately not," Wilder continued. He patted his wife's hand as he talked, soothing her along with himself. "When Eve was at school, she had trouble focusing. And some nights she couldn't sleep. Yet she'd say she didn't feel tired the next day. Other nights, we could barely wake her in the morning. She'd tell us she was exhausted and had no energy. She'd complain of stomach aches, headaches… all sorts of aches and pains."

"You have to realize," Phoebe inserted. "Eve was doted on growing up. We loved her… we *love* her... dearly. Wilder and I, along with her three big brothers, showered Eve with attention and positive reinforcement. We couldn't figure out what was wrong when she started acting strange… Or I guess I should say… exhibiting symptoms."

"I get that," Luke confirmed. "You don't have to convince me, folks. I can see the love in this family. It's obvious."

That reassurance gave them all a measure of comfort, one that they sorely needed.

"Keep going," Luke said to Wilder, flattening one of his big, brown hands on the table. "This is very helpful. You're doing great. And listen, I have daughters myself. Twin daughters, actually. I get it. We'd do anything for our kids."

"Okay," Wilder responded, cracking a couple of knuckles again. The motion seemed to help him gather his thoughts, and his courage. "Going on… Her senior year at East Valley High, Eve started acting impulsively. The first thing that happened that was way out of character for her was shoplifting. She stole more than a hundred dollar's worth of clothes from Decker's even though she had plenty of money to pay for them. It was like she wanted the thrill of the risk."

"She was promptly caught, thankfully," Phoebe added. "The department store called us rather than the police since Eve was underage and it was her first offense."

"Yeah," Wilder continued. "That much was good, but it was only the beginning. Next up was stealing our checkbook and writing checks all over town. And I don't mean writing checks for things she needed to buy like clothes or groceries. She was writing checks to strangers we didn't know. We finally figured out she was buying alcohol in a roundabout way. It didn't even make sense. She would write a check to some stranger who would then go buy the alcohol for her. But like… why a check? She could have easily used cash. It was like she wanted us to catch her."

"That's what we thought…" Phoebe filled in. "Except I'm still not sure whether it was a cry for help. She had so much trouble making decisions, or even thinking straight at all."

"Right," Wilder said. "All of that quickly led to more bad decisions including drinking and driving, unprotected sex with scary people, and…" He choked up and couldn't get the words out.

Phoebe leaned towards her husband and gripped his hand tightly. She tried to speak, but couldn't do it either.

Holden placed a hand on each of his parents, then gave breath to what they hadn't mentioned since the day it happened.

Luke lowered his eyebrows, hurting with the Blackburns as he listened. He'd read the file. He knew what was coming.

"And then, she attempted suicide…" Holden's face contorted. He struggled to keep his composure. "She did it in such dramatic fashion... An innocent young man lost his life…"

14

___

Eve woke up groggy. She wasn't sure how long she had been out... Asleep... or unconscious. The uncertainty scared her.

For a moment, Eve remembered being a young child and waking up in bed beside her mother. She remembered the pink gingham print on her favorite childhood pajamas. They were the footed kind with a long white zipper up the front and a hood. She remembered her favorite stuffed animal, a penguin named Polly her parents had gotten her on a trip to the zoo in Portland. Eve had slept with that penguin until she was nearly a teenager. She remembered the cool slosh of her parents' king-size waterbed, a holdout from the eighties. They had kept the thing long after waterbeds were out of style.

It felt like Eve might be a child again, right there with her mother and Polly, if only she closed her eyes tightly and wished hard enough. Eve longed for that feeling of safety and security. She needed it now more than ever.

It took her a while to get her bearings.

Slowly, she remembered Saul. And their house party. But she was terribly confused. Furniture and windows whizzed by in a blur as her eyes struggled to make sense of what she was seeing. A TV blared a laugh track from somewhere in the distance.

It was still dark outside. That much was clear. Although Eve wasn't sure it was the same night. Time felt strange, like perhaps this was an entirely different night. She couldn't say with certainty how long she had been out. This, too, scared her.

She rolled onto her side to look around and felt something heavy drop out of her hand. She squinted her eyes as she scanned the scene. She was in Saul's living room. On his brown upholstered sofa. Her body ached, apparently from sleeping in a contorted position.

Eve wanted to call out for Tim, but didn't want to hurt Saul's feelings. She thought she was supposed to be with Saul now, and she figured she shouldn't mention any other man. She reiterated the thought that she had to give Saul what he wanted. She honestly didn't believe she had any other choice.

This made Eve sad. Overwhelmingly so. She tried her best to choke back the tears that threatened to spring from her eyes. Her feelings were a jumble. She hated when they got that way.

Her head pounded again. Only this time, her mouth was dry and tasted like vomit. So dry that it felt like she'd been outside on a hot day without water. The taste of vomit wasn't nearly as uncomfortable as the dryness.

Her skin was itchy, as if creepy crawlies had been all over it. She wanted to scratch, but couldn't, for some reason. She wondered if bugs had been on her while she slept. Roaches, probably. Or bedbugs. Saul's place didn't look dirty enough to have roaches or bedbugs, but it wasn't clean like Eve's own home. Tim had made sure that things were kept clean and orderly there. Eve didn't like bugs, but she felt too disconnected from the physical sensation of itchiness to do much about it. She mentally shelved that particular concern, telling herself she'd look for bug bites later.

Eve's attention shifted back to whatever it was that she dropped. Something about it alarmed her. She tried to reach over the edge of the sofa. But her limbs were numb and uncooperative. They seemed to be moving without her permission or control when they moved at all. This concerned her most of all. She'd been through a lot in her young life, but throughout it all, she had maintained use of her limbs.

Panicked, Eve used all of her energy to thrust herself over the side of the sofa and onto the floor below. She had to see what she had dropped. It was all she could focus on. Maybe the object would help anchor her. Maybe she could figure out how to center herself. She felt very afraid of what might happen otherwise. Her anxiety was escalating with each passing second.

Eve landed on the floor with a thud, and to her horror, found the now familiar object in front of her face. Her eyes struggled to focus. They crossed, then spread, working to function.

It was a shiny, silver knife, lying in plain sight between Eve and the bottom of the sofa. She couldn't be sure of its size, but it wasn't small. It looked like a butcher knife of some sort. Big enough to do major damage against soft human flesh. On it, dull and dried, were swirly splotches of blood.

Eve instantly knew this knife was the object she had been holding. She knew it, like she knew her own name. And she knew that the splotches were indeed blood. Not ketchup. Not wine. Blood. She had a memory that told her so. She forced it back.

What have I done? Oh, my God. What have I done?!

Eve screamed, but only vomit came out. It was forceful, her body trying to rid itself of the poison she had put in. She wretched and heaved, the acid burning her throat as it came up. Barf pooled around her head and piled up on the beige carpet. It was a ridiculous amount.

Eve wondered where it had come from. It felt like it had come from someone else. Disconnected and foreign.

Finally, after what felt like an eternity in a battle with her own digestive tract and the abuse she had dealt it, Eve stopped vomiting long enough to assess her situation further.

Her limbs still numb and unwieldy, she managed to roll away from the sofa with another few thrusts of her body.

Away from the vomit. And away from the bloody knife.

As she came to a stop, facing the other direction, Eve's gaze landed on Saul. He was lying on the floor in front of her. His eyes were open, staring up at the ceiling. His skin was the strangest shades of purple and blue. Vomit was piled up next to his head as well, soaking his hair and the collar of his shirt.

The scene was disgusting. Revolting. Assaulting to every single one of the senses.

"Saul!" she cried, though she couldn't be sure any sound was coming out at all. "Saul! Answer me, Saul. I beg you."

Eve resisted admitting what she already knew, wiping her eyes as tears poured.

She thrashed her body around, slamming into Saul's and begging him to wake up. She cried and pleaded. She prayed. He didn't respond.

Finally, Eve looked hard at his rigid face and accepted the reality of the situation.

Saul Milton was dead and gone.

15

Never before had Eve been so distraught. And that was saying something.

Traumas had piled up on her, thick and heavy. Like tar. Or maybe quicksand. The visual wasn't as important as the hopelessness of it all. She didn't know how she would ever get herself out and breathe freely again.

As she stared as Saul's dead body, Eve's brain played cruel tricks on her. Her vision blurry, his facial features swirled around in her mind's eye until she was seeing her beloved Tim instead. She saw Tim lifeless. Unresponsive. Unmoving. Dead and gone.

"Tim!" she called. "Tim! Wake up, Tim. I need you. You can't leave me like this."

She sobbed and heaved as she yelled, her voice rising higher and higher over the television.

"Tim! I can't go on without you. I don't *want* to go on without you."

Eve closed her eyes, tears bursting through the cracks. Her limbs were still numb. She could hardly move. She was stuck there on the floor, beside what she now saw as Tim's dead body.

"This isn't fair!" she yelled as loud as she could, eyes pressed shut. "I want out. I don't want to be here!"

She jerked her shoulders and kicked her head backwards as she yelled, flailing around wildly. She needed to do something to calm herself down, and quick.

As Eve continued to press her eyelids together tightly, memories flooded her consciousness. She saw herself with Tim during some of their happiest times. She leaned into the happy memories, hoping they would help her escape her current reality.

She saw the day she met Tim in vivid color. It had been a good day. One of her best.

Eve had recently returned home after college graduation and was having lunch with her parents at Brick House Cafe in downtown Rosemary Run when she bumped into Tim... literally. She stood up out of a booth on her way to the restroom as he was following the hostess to his table. They collided in an almost comical fashion, like a scene from a romcom. Eve's phone and purse went crashing to the floor, as did the satchel full of papers Tim was holding. They bent down to pick their things up at the same time, and their eyes met. The rest was history.

Eve had felt good in those days. Her meds were working well for you. She felt... almost normal.

As she remembered now, Eve let herself become immersed in the scene. She could see Tim's face, his cheeks pink with embarrassment and his eyes alight with interest. He had seemed shy and reserved, but Eve knew immediately that he liked her. He looked like a young professor. That day, he had been wearing a tweed sport coat over a neatly pressed shirt that was accented by leather suspenders and a navy blue bowtie. He had a quirky charm Eve found appealing.

Closing her eyes tighter, she could almost feel the warm May air from that day. The air had been easy and comfortable, with all the promise of summer. Eve could hear the gentle sway of the trees in the courtyard outside the cafe, windows open to let the breeze in. She could smell the food, the aroma of freshly baked bread and meats wafting throughout the dining room.

She remembered the softness and warmth of Tim's hand as he introduced himself and shook hers.

Life had seemed positive then. Full of possibility. She'd had her parents to keep her grounded. And her therapist.

Eve thought maybe she should call them now. One of them. But who?

Forcing that idea out of her mind as quickly as it had entered, she moved on to whatever happy memory she could access.

Think.

Before long, the memory of the day Tim had asked Eve to marry him came into full view.

The couple had been hiking on a crisp fall day, less than six months after they'd met and began dating. The leaves on the trees were brilliant oranges and yellows. Seeing the leaves up close and feeling them crunch underfoot were a special treat since the lower elevations in town didn't get the same fall foliage. Tim had packed a picnic lunch complete with little sandwiches, wine, and cheese. It was the perfect wine country outing.

As Eve was spreading out a plaid blanket on the side of the grassy hill, she had turned around to find Tim down on one knee, a diamond ring in his hand. The stone sparkled in the afternoon sunshine, lit up nearly as brightly as Tim's smile. He beamed as he told Eve that he would give her his heart forever if she'd be his wife. He said he wanted to be with her for all the days of his life, to love and protect her. In sickness and in health. In good times and in bad. He said he'd hold her in his arms, right where she belonged.

She had said yes. Enthusiastically, *yes*.

If only Tim were here to hold and protect her now.

The pain of missing him was too much.

Eve opened her eyes, remembering the knife. If her hands would work to hold it, she could use the blade to end things.

Without Tim, she didn't want to go on. Her life had been a series of trials ever since her terrible disease had taken over her mind and body when she was a teenager. Eve had hurt and disappointed people and she didn't want to do it any longer. She was certain that her parents and brothers would be better off without her. She was a smear on their honorable lives full of productivity and balance. She was a thorn in their sides. A burden. A problem. A *freak*.

And besides, if Tim wasn't on this Earth anymore, maybe she could go wherever he was. Maybe he would hold and protect her there. He loved her truly. She knew that. Maybe they weren't meant to be apart, like he'd said in his vows on their wedding day, Eve dressed in flowing white as the summer breeze blew through her red hair.

Maybe it was their destiny to live short lives. Maybe the best was yet to come in whatever was next.

Eve blinked, willing her eyes to focus as she looked around for the knife.

She knew how she'd use it. She wouldn't fool with slicing her wrists like often depicted in horror movies. She wanted to be sure the job was done, and that she didn't suffer long. She'd drive the blade deep into her throat.

And then she'd lay back, waiting for Tim to come and take her into his arms.

16

Temperatures were falling when Margaret's plane landed in Rosemary Run, just before midnight local time. Her flight had been delayed leaving Phoenix due to high winds from the approaching cold front, which was already disrupting air travel along the West Coast. She was glad to have made it before the snow.

Margaret was exhausted. She wasn't a young woman.

She'd given birth to Tim when she was in her early forties, making her nearly a decade older than Wilder and Phoebe. Tim had been a late-in-life surprise. Margaret had thought she'd never have children, but Tim was a welcome addition. He was her one and only.

Unfortunately, heartbreak had been in store for the Fischer family. Tim's father died of an aggressive cancer when Tim was in elementary school. Margaret did her best as a single mother, but she and Tim struggled to connect ever since. Their relationship was friendly, but they didn't have a lot in common.

Margaret wished things could be different. She hoped there would still be time.

Holden and his parents were waiting at the gate when Margaret stepped off the bridge. The Rosemary Run airport was small enough to allow for such conveniences. Their security protocols were more relaxed due to the small volume of passengers they served.

Margaret stumbled on the uneven surface where the bridge connected to the terminal floor, her athletic shoes appearing too big for her feet. Not to mention, she was bogged down by several large bags and an unwieldy neck pillow. Holden rushed forward to assist.

"Mrs. Fischer, let me help you with those," he said.

It took Margaret by surprise. Apparently, she hadn't been expecting the Blackburns to be there.

"Holden," she said with a weary smile. "I didn't know I'd be seeing you tonight. Thank you for coming. I thought you'd be home with Lorelei and the kids."

"You're family," he said as he took the bags out of her hands. "Mom and Dad are here too. We'll drive you. And you're welcome to stay with us if you like. Between the lot of us, we have several spare bedrooms."

"That's very kind," Margaret replied, moving to a row of chairs away from the flow of traffic. "And please, call me Margaret."

Wilder and Phoebe walked over to join them, smiling as much as they could under the circumstances.

"Hello, Margaret," Wilder said, reaching out to give her a hug. Phoebe followed her husband's lead, making it a group hug.

Suddenly choked up, Margaret was overwhelmed and speechless.

"We're glad you're here," Phoebe offered. "I'm just sorry… You know…"

Margaret nodded, then pulled a bunched up tissue from her handbag and blotted at her eyes. "Thank you," she managed. "It's very nice of you folks to meet me here like this."

"I told her," Holden inserted. "We're family."

"That's right," Phoebe confirmed.

Margaret smiled, her sadness mixed with appreciation.

Holden looked at his parents, again willing to take the lead, but not wanting to overstep. Wilder winked in his son's direction, giving him the okay to go ahead.

"Do you need anything before we get into the car?" Holden asked Margaret. "Food? Something to drink?"

Margaret shook her head. "Gosh, I couldn't eat a thing if I wanted to."

"I know the feeling," Phoebe agreed. "The detectives practically had to force food down our throats earlier. But I'm glad they did. I feel a lot stronger since I had something to eat."

"Are you sure we can't get you something?" Holden asked. "How about a little protein? A packet of peanuts maybe?"

Margaret seemed like she wanted to protest, but she knew they were right. She should eat. She'd need her strength. "Sure," she said. "Thank you, Holden. Peanuts will do."

"Good," he confirmed, taking Margaret's hand and

leading her to a chair. "Have a seat here and I'll run to the shop around the corner. Is water okay to drink?"

"Yes. Thank you. Truly."

"It's no problem," Holden confirmed. He turned to face his parents. "Mom? Dad? Can I get you anything?"

"No," they said in unison.

"We'll stay here with Margaret," Phoebe added.

As Holden left for the peanuts, Margaret plopped down in the chair. "This kind of thing is tough on old folks like me," she said lightly, trying to ease the tense mood. But a light mood wasn't right, and she couldn't keep up the facade for even a minute. Her face fell, and she began to cry again.

"We're right there with you," Wilder said. "Although we didn't have to fly from Phoenix, of course. How was your flight?"

"It was fine," she replied. "I'm here in one piece, so that's what matters…"

As she said it, all three of them bristled. They wished Eve and Tim were there. In one piece.

"I'm sorry," Margaret offered. "I'm not sure what to say or do. Please, forgive me."

"No apology necessary," Wilder said.

"What should we do?" Margaret asked.

Wilder and Phoebe glanced at each other. They had been debating this themselves. James had told them it was okay to search. They knew they needed rest, but they felt bad going home to bed when Eve and Tim were out there somewhere, possibly in serious danger.

"What?" Margaret prompted. "Fill me in, please."

"We're just…" Phoebe stammered. "We're not sure

what to do with ourselves. We're bone tired already, but we feel guilty going to sleep."

"Ah," Margaret said, taking off her eyeglasses and folding them up in one hand. "I don't know the answer to that either. I don't know where we'd start if we were going to stay up tonight. Maybe we should sleep awhile and then get going bright and early."

"Maybe," Phoebe agreed.

"Wait," Margaret continued. "You have a resort to run. Do you have to go there in the morning?"

"Goodness, no," Phoebe replied. "We don't care about anything but finding Tim and Eve. Business is just that. It's not our top priority."

"Besides," Wilder added. "We have a well-trained staff who can hold down the fort. They can handle most things. So…"

Holden walked up with the peanuts and water for Margaret before Wilder could finish. "Who can handle what?" he asked.

"The resort," Wilder explained. "I was telling Margaret it isn't important right now."

"Right," Holden said, handing the haggard woman the snack.

Margaret smiled her thanks, then ate the peanuts hungrily. She had needed them more than she realized. When she was finished, she balled the wrapper up and put it into a pocket on the outside of one of her bags.

"Can I sleep at Tim's house?" she blurted. "I mean… Tim and Eve's? I… I guess I want to feel close to my son."

Margaret's pointed remark made Phoebe tear up. She could only imagine what this situation would be like with a strained parent-child relationship. Phoebe had experienced difficulties with Eve from time to time. But for the most part, they were close. And they had a large family to lean on. Phoebe felt sorry for Margaret.

"I think that will be okay," Holden confirmed. "There's an officer stationed outside. You'll be safe there."

Wilder and Phoebe agreed.

Margaret nodded, grateful. She looked determined now. "Good. Will you take me there?"

"Right away," Holden replied. "Do you have a checked bag that we need to pick up at baggage claim?"

"Nope. Everything I brought is right here." She gestured to the bags, seeming proud of her own efficiency. "Let's sleep," Margaret continued. "I can't imagine what we could do to help in the middle of the night, anyway. We'll reconvene first thing in the morning. Maybe the police will have a lead by then. Maybe Tim and Eve will be home..."

The Blackburns reluctantly agreed. They knew Margaret was right. And they had said much the same to the rest of the family. They all needed rest.

Slowly, they walked with Margaret out of the airport, then they helped her climb into the passenger seat of Holden's SUV.

Margaret seemed frail under the moonlight, pained by years of loneliness and regret. It was sad to witness. Her knuckles were enlarged from arthritis. Her skin wrinkled and thin. And the lines on her face seemed deep and burdensome.

Phoebe wondered if Margaret could handle what might come. She wondered the same about herself.

Holden drove, taking Margaret to Tim and Eve's house. He got her inside and comfortable, then took his parents home. It all felt surreal, like they were part of a bad movie that they hadn't asked to star in. They certainly couldn't have predicted this end to the day when they had woken up that morning, tending to business as usual.

Finally, Holden returned to his own house. He curled up beside Lorelei in bed and wrapped his arms tightly around her.

No one slept much, though they tried. They tucked into their beds and closed their eyes, waiting for a new day and hoping it would bring them good news.

17

The sun peeked above the horizon when the family gathered at Tim and Eve's house to start the next day. They were scheduled to meet with Detectives Fredericks and Hemming at the police station at eight. They intended to formulate plans of their own before then. They were determined that today would be a productive one.

"I had a dream," Phoebe announced when everyone was gathered in the living room.

Wilder was by her side, clasping her hand tightly. He apparently knew his wife would make the announcement, because he didn't look surprised.

"Tell us," Marcus said eagerly.

He and Ty had dropped Bethany off to spend the day at Lorelei and Holden's house. Lorelei and Imogen had promised to keep all the little ones fed and happy so the other adults in the bunch could focus on finding Tim and Eve.

"Yeah," Jake echoed. "What was it, Mom?"

Victoria had stayed home this morning, promising to join them later in the day. She had promised to keep a careful watch on Eve's social media accounts.

Margaret looked surprisingly refreshed. The Blackburns thought she must be a morning person. They were impressed by how quickly she revived.

"I think the dream meant something," Phoebe continued. "It was… heavy."

"Well, spill it," Margaret said. "With all due respect, Phoebe, this isn't time for sugarcoating."

Phoebe nodded. "It was Tim."

The statement took Margaret by surprise. Tears sprang to her eyes. "What about Tim?"

Holden nodded, encouraging his mom to continue.

"It wasn't about Tim… as much as it *was* Tim. He came to me in a dream," Phoebe claimed. "And… he told me Eve was in grave danger."

"What?" Jake said, rattled.

"I know," Phoebe replied. "It was short and simple. He said we must find Eve. That she's in danger. I got the idea that time is running out."

Tension was heavy in the room. It was as if everyone was suddenly spooked.

"But…" Margaret began. "What about Tim? What does that mean for him? For my… my boy."

Phoebe looked down at the floor, choking back tears.

Wilder took over. "It's a dream. That's all."

Phoebe raised a hand, stopping her husband from discounting it so quickly. She knew he believed in her intuition. But she also knew he was trying to ease Margaret's mind.

"I don't care," Margaret said, her voice rising. "Phoebe, what do you think that means about Tim? Is he in danger too?"

Phoebe leaned against the back of the sofa she was sitting on, almost shaking.

"Mom," Holden began, offering an out. "We could talk more about your dream later. We have logistics to go over and not a lot of time before we need to be at the police station."

Phoebe's boys knew her well enough to understand her interpretation of the dream. She didn't have to spell it out for them. They knew she'd had several dreams over the years where people who had recently passed away came back to communicate with her. No one still alive ever had. Even Marcus knew, having been filled in by his husband.

Margaret was the only one in the dark.

Poor Margaret.

"No!" she said forcefully. "I won't be coddled. I buried a husband and raised our son alone. I'm tougher than I look. Now tell me what you mean to say, Phoebe."

"Okay, Margaret," the Blackburn matriarch said, acquiescing. "I think it means that Tim has passed."

"Passed?" Margaret blurted. "As in… he's dead?"

"I'm so sorry," Phoebe replied. "Yes."

Margaret scooted to the front edge of her armchair, her face twisted up, her finger pointing. She looked angry and sad all at the same time. "How…? Why… I…?"

"She's had these dreams over the years," Holden explained. "Mom has dreamed of people who have passed away. Several of them. She seems to have a sixth sense about that kind of thing."

"An open line of communication, if you will," Wilder added.

Margaret leaned her head down into her hands. She sat silently like that for what felt to the others like an eternity. They didn't want to disturb her. They didn't know what she was doing. Finally, she raised her head and sat up stick straight in her chair, her hands gripping the armrests.

"I'm sorry," Phoebe repeated. "You have to know… we love Tim like a son. I don't take this lightly. I'm devastated."

"Stop," Margaret said. "Don't go there. I know how you feel about my son. He's told me how wonderful you all are."

"He's the best," Holden added.

"We couldn't have asked for a better husband for our Eve," Wilder confirmed. "What a guy."

Margaret nodded, her face brave. "How did he look?" she asked Phoebe.

"You mean…?"

"In your dream. How did my boy look?"

Phoebe sniffled, emotion full on her face. "He looked good. He was whole. And safe… if that's what you mean. He was very worried about Eve. Adamant that we *had* to find her."

"Did he give you any clues as to how we could do that?" Margaret asked.

"No."

Margaret laced her fingers together, twisting a ring

around one arthritic finger as she worked to hold her hurt inside. "Did he say… what happened to him?" She barely got the words out before devolving into a puddle of tears.

Holden handed Margaret a tissue from his chair near hers. He had a pocket full of them, expecting to need them today.

"He didn't," Phoebe explained. "In my experience though, I often have a series of dreams when someone comes to me like this. Maybe he'll come back again."

Margaret eyed her curiously.

"Maybe we'll learn something when we meet with the detectives," Holden offered. "I'm sure they have new information to share by now."

"You mean, maybe they'll confirm that my son's dead?" Margaret said.

She was raw, blunt and without tact. No one blamed her.

"Maybe," Holden confirmed. "I sure hope not. But I know we all want answers. Not knowing is the worst."

Margaret stood up, then plodded her way across the living room towards the guest room where she had spent the night, stepping over people as she went. "Excuse me," she said. "I need a few minutes."

"Of course," Wilder said. "Take your time."

"Please, let us know if we can do anything at all for you, Mrs. Fischer," Ty said.

"It's Margaret," she mumbled, then closed and locked the door behind her.

The mood was heavy amongst the others. Assuming Phoebe's dream was right, they mourned for Tim, and they feared that Eve didn't have much time.

"Holden," Jake began. "You're our leader. Mom and Dad are in too much pain to think straight. Tell us what to do."

"Yeah," Ty confirmed. "How can we help?"

"Count me in," Marcus added. "I'm at your service. I want to help."

Phoebe and Wilder were touched as they watched their boys in action. Even without their parental input, the boys functioned like a well-oiled machine, all doing their part.

If only they could somehow help Eve. Maybe they still could.

"Do your best, Holden," Wilder said. "If you're up to the task, we believe in you. Give us our marching orders."

Holden nodded. "I'm up for it," he confirmed. "I appreciate your faith in me. All of you… It's an honor."

"It's well deserved, son," Wilder said, wiping a tear from his eye.

"Okay, then," Holden continued. "Here's what I'm thinking…"

The Blackburns moved forward in their seats, eager to hear what Holden had in mind. They were desperate to *do* something. They had waited around for far too long.

Jake took out a notebook to take notes.

"To begin, it's simple," Holden said. "We'll go to the police department and hear what the detectives have to tell us. Then, assuming a search is still underway, we fan out and start talking to everyone we can. We'll hit the streets with posters, we'll hit the phones, and we'll spread word all over the internet."

"I'll handle the internet," Jake offered. "I'll get

Victoria to help. We'll spread their pictures far and wide, asking for any information."

"Good," Holden said to his brother. The two of them worked well together at Brambleberry Fields. It made sense that they'd do so again in this setting. "The police may have generated a graphic already. If not, I'll need you to do that. Find recent pictures of Tim and Eve to share. Be sure they're well lit and show their faces clearly. You'll want to make sure the information gets around town, and also around the Florida Keys and San Francisco. We want to hear from anyone who may have seen them."

"Understood," Jake confirmed. "I'll look around the house now for recent pictures that I don't already have digital copies of."

"We will take care of the posters," Ty offered. Marcus nodded his agreement.

"Great," Holden said. "It will be good to have two of you on that."

"I assume we can use the same pictures of their faces that Jake will post on the Internet, correct?" Ty asked.

"That's right," Holden confirmed. "Make the posters colorful, so they stand out. I'm thinking neon colors, actually. Pink, yellow, orange, and lime green. Put 'MISSING' in big letters on the front with their pictures and the phone number of the Rosemary Run Police Department tip line."

"Got it," Ty confirmed.

"That reminds me," Holden continued. "I think we should offer a reward for information leading to their whereabouts. Does anyone object to that?"

"Not at all," Wilder said. "I was going to mention the

same thing myself. We have the means. We should use what we have."

"I agree," Holden replied. "I'm happy to pitch in personal funds. Dad, how much are you thinking?"

Wilder tilted his head to one side. "Son, I'd give up every dollar I had if it would bring Eve back to us."

"Damn right, you would," Phoebe added. "But we don't want to go overboard and turn this into a ransom situation for anyone who may find her. Perhaps we should ask the detectives for guidance."

"Good idea," Wilder confirmed. "People can get crazy when there's money involved. We don't want somebody grabbing Eve just for the payday. Or worse yet, asking for more than we can provide. Although, granted, that would be a lot."

This was one of the times that the Blackburns felt fortunate to have achieved such a high level of success in business. Thanks to the fortune earned through Brambleberry Fields, they were equipped to pay a reward that could help them find Eve.

"I guess that leaves your dad and me on the phones," Phoebe said. "Which is fine. Maybe we could do it from here. And maybe Margaret will want to help."

"Sounds good, Mom," Holden confirmed. "There's plenty of room here. If volunteers from the community want to help, let them. This house can be the official headquarters for those working the phones."

"Same for the Internet," Jake added. "I can do what I need to from here. We have enough bandwidth for several other Internet-savvy volunteers to help me. Let's ask the community."

"Ask people to help distribute posters, too," Ty added. "We will take all the help we can get."

"Okay then," Holden confirmed. "Those will be the three main ways we get the word out. If there's anything else or any more specifics to share, I'll divvy those up as needed."

"Good work, Holden," Phoebe said. "Now let's get Margaret and head to the station. That is, if she feels up to going after what I said. I hope I haven't offended her. It didn't feel right to remain silent about my dream."

"I don't think you had much choice, Mom," Holden said. "We need to use every bit of insight available to us. And your dream is insightful, whether everyone wants to believe that or not."

Resolute, the Blackburns gathered their things and got in the car, ready to hear whatever news awaited them at the police station. They felt better with a plan of action. They were growing more and more worried about Eve. But they knew missing person situations sometimes took a while. They would keep at it until she was found.

Holden was about to knock on the door to the guest room when Margaret opened it, her purse and coat in hand.

"Are you coming with us?" he asked. "Because you don't have to. You could stay here and we could report back. You must be tired after the last-minute travel and late night."

"I'm coming with you," she said. "I couldn't live with myself if I didn't. Now let's go, so we're not late for the detectives."

18

———

The mood was somber at the police station when they arrived. Pamela was there and offered them coffee, but she didn't smile. Her face looked heavy under the weight of the things she'd seen. No one envied her, or any of the other individuals on the local force.

The Blackburns could immediately tell that Neil and Luke had bad news to deliver. Given Phoebe's dream, they suspected that it might be about Tim. Phoebe put a protective hand on Margaret's back as they were shown into the same conference room they'd occupied the evening before.

After Margaret was introduced to everyone, she urged them to get down to business.

"We have news," Luke said, the words hanging in the air. His face was emotionless. Official. "Are you ready to hear it?"

"We're as ready as we'll ever be," Holden said, speaking for the group. "We're scared, but we have to know."

Luke glanced at Margaret for confirmation.

"Go ahead," she said.

Luke opened the file folder in front of him and placed his palms flat on the table on either side. Neil sat next to his partner, arms hanging in his lap. His face looked official too, but like he had a harder time appearing emotionless. Neil's eyes were narrowed and his brow was low. His bottom lip seemed like it could tremble at any moment.

"We don't have any news about Eve," Luke began. "She's still considered missing. We're doing everything we can to find her."

Phoebe exhaled loudly, unable to hold the breath in any longer.

"And Tim?" Margaret asked, her bottom lip firm.

Neil looked down.

Luke spoke.

"I regret to inform you that Tim Fischer was killed in Islamorada, Florida on Thursday. It was a jet ski accident."

Margaret yelped and threw both hands up to her mouth, as if to hold the sound in.

"It was reportedly a freak accident," Luke continued. "Tim's jet ski collided with a boat. He was killed instantly. He didn't suffer."

Phoebe, Wilder, and Holden reached their hands toward Margaret, comforting her with pats on the arms and shoulders. She looked stunned.

"Tim didn't have identification on him when he was killed," Luke continued. "His body was held at the office of the Monroe County, Florida medical examiner in

Marathon. He was registered as a John Doe. Our inquiry yesterday led to a positive identification."

"Wait!" Margaret shouted. "Are you sure it's him? Maybe it's someone else… How?"

"We're sure," Luke replied. "Confirmed with dental records. I'm sorry, Mrs. Fischer."

Margaret sank low into her chair. "Call me Margaret," she mumbled. Her eyes glazed over as she stared at a random spot on the cement-block wall near the door.

"Was the driver of the boat at fault?" Holden inquired.

"Local police don't think so. Alcohol and drugs were not involved. The male boat driver was tested. He was clean."

"Was the driver injured?" Holden asked.

"Minor injuries," Luke replied, glancing at a note in the file folder. "He was treated and released the same day."

"Wow," Wilder said. "And Eve?"

Neil took a deep breath. Luke looked to him for an answer.

The two of them had split duties so Luke led the investigation into Tim's whereabouts and Neil headed up the search for Eve.

"We don't know," Neil replied. "We know she was with Tim on the beach at the resort before he boarded the jet ski. We can assume she was still in the vicinity when he was killed. She probably saw the collision from the beach. We're still piecing together a timeline…"

Luke jumped in. "Eve disappeared at some point after the incident and wasn't seen again on the resort's security cameras until Sunday morning when she checked out, as scheduled. If she was there when paramedics arrived, she didn't identify herself. A crowd had gathered."

Margaret shook her head. "She was right. Damn her."

"Right about what? Who?" Neil asked, curious.

"Phoebe," Margaret said, slinging a hand in her direction. "She knew Tim was dead."

Holden sighed as the detectives took note of the changing dynamics within the group. Luke and Neil were trained to spot irregularities in human behavior. It was their duty to watch for anything suspicious. They perked up, waiting to hear more.

"What do you mean?" Luke asked. "No one knew. We just got confirmation from the Florida medical examiner a few hours ago."

"She did," Margaret insisted, throwing Phoebe and Wilder's hands off. "She says Tim came to her in a dream last night where he told her Eve was in danger. Do you believe that? Because I think it's a load of horseshit."

Luke stared at her curiously.

Margaret continued. "I, for one, would like to hear what else Phoebe Blackburn is privy to. How can we be sure she wasn't involved? I don't know her. Not really. But I'll bet she'd do anything for her precious Eve, that psychotic little bitch. I'll bet my son would be alive right now if he hadn't gotten involved with Eve. She is certifiably crazy. The apple probably doesn't fall far from the tree. Not from what I've seen."

Wilder stood up, raising his hands in the air. "Whoa, whoa, now," he said forcefully. "Emotions are high. We get that. But my wife had nothing to do with this. And… there's no reason to speak ill of our daughter. Please."

"Eve can't help how she is," Phoebe pleaded, not bothering to defend herself. She could let the insults slung in her direction slide, but she couldn't ignore those about Eve. "No more than anyone else with a mental illness can. She doesn't deserve to be called names."

Phoebe felt protective of Eve. Any parent would. Wilder certainly did, too.

"Especially when she isn't here to defend herself," Wilder added. "I mean, really." He rumpled his face, anger coursing through his veins.

Luke and Neil remained silent, watching and listening.

"And now we know why Tim and his mother weren't close," Jake muttered.

Those were fighting words.

Margaret leaned forward in her chair. "Detectives," she said. "I want my son's death investigated thoroughly. I think foul play may have been involved."

"Oh, come on, Margaret," Holden inserted. "That's ridiculous. You heard the detectives. It was an accident. A horrible, terrible accident. Let's not turn on each other. We're all grieving for Tim."

"Easy for you to say," Margaret quipped. "You're the golden boy, born with a silver spoon in your mouth. You wouldn't dare speak against a member of the Blackburn family, even if it was the truth."

"Not so…" Holden replied. "Not. So."

Phoebe's voice rattled as she talked, she was so upset. She turned to face Margaret. "You have no idea what it's like to have a close family member who is mentally ill…

To have a child who is mentally ill, who won't ever be able to fully care for themselves. It sucks the soul right out of you. All the waiting for something bad to happen. The fear about the trauma your child is experiencing on any given day. Not to mention, the fear about whether you'll be able to handle whatever happens. And the rage... The rage is the worst, because you don't want this to be your life. Only it is. There's no cure. No permanent fix. No escape..."

"Maybe I don't," Margaret replied. "All of my close family members are dead. So, sorry if I'm not joining your little pity party. Your family members are still alive. The whole— what, *dozen?*— of them. Do you realize how insensitive you sound right now, Phoebe? How arrogant? I just learned that my only son is dead."

"Alright," Neil interrupted. "That's enough, folks. This isn't helping anyone."

"You can say that again," Margaret replied. "I came all the way from Phoenix, only to be disrespected. And caught up in this family's soap opera."

"*Enough*," Neil emphasized.

The group sat quietly, pondering.

"Mrs. Fischer— *Margaret*— we have a grief counselor on staff we'd like you to speak with," Neil continued. "Are you willing? His name is Robert Jordan."

"I don't know," Margaret said. "What good would it do?"

"Aside from your emotional needs, there are a number of decisions that will have to be made. Like about Tim's remains. And his funeral. Robert can help guide you, and he can connect you with local resources. You'll want to speak with an attorney about your rights and any potential inheritance."

"Oh," Margaret replied. "I see. I wasn't thinking that far."

"How about you come with me?" Neil asked. "We'll let the Blackburns discuss the search for Eve while you focus on Tim. I think that's best right now."

Neil felt like a kindergarten teacher wrangling irritable children. He felt for them. Luke did, too. But there was business to tend to, and there wasn't time to waste. His actions or lack thereof could mean the difference between life and death for Eve. Neil had a duty to make every minute count for her.

Neil didn't have biological children of his own, but he was raising three step-children along with his wife Cate. He could hardly imagine the pain and anguish he would go through if one of them were missing, especially if they had a mental illness like Eve. Neil also understood how the love and concern a parent has for a child goes on even after they become adults.

In that vein and at the same time, Neil felt sad for Margaret. He wanted her to be in the caring hands of someone who could help ease her pain during this most difficult time. Next to the day her husband died, this had to be the worst day of her life.

Robert was a good grief counselor and a good man. Neil knew that he would take good care of Margaret. Placing her into his care was the best thing to do. He hoped that removing her from the room didn't drive a further wedge between Margaret and the Blackburn family.

"Okay," Margaret agreed. "I'll talk to the grief counselor. Let's go. I could use some privacy to clear my head, anyway."

She stood up and left the room without so much as making eye contact with any of the Blackburns.

19

When Margaret was gone, the Blackburns began talking amongst themselves. They were comfortable again and needed to tend to their family's business without unnecessary drama.

"Can you believe her?" Jake asked, in a rare instance of speaking up without waiting for Holden or his parents to take the lead. "That was completely uncalled for. And downright rude. I almost said some things I might have regretted. Or maybe I wouldn't regret them at all. I seriously understand why Tim wasn't close to her. I'd like to..."

"No need," Holden said, giving a stern look to his little brother.

"Yeah, I'm with you, Jake," Marcus added. "I was about to…"

"Me too," Ty said to his husband. "How dare she talk about Mom and Eve like that?" He balled up one fist and raised it toward his face.

"Mhm," Marcus replied. "Ugly. That's what we call

that kind of behavior where I'm from... Acting ugly. That old woman should be ashamed of herself."

"Right," Jake added. "We can't help it she's bitter. She's apparently mad at the world. Probably has been ever since her husband died when Tim was a kid. I get that she's experienced loss, but how did she become so nasty?"

"Maybe she was always that way," Ty added. "Maybe it isn't the loss."

"Maybe she's jealous of how close Tim was to us," Holden reasoned. "Or maybe she's just tired and irritable. There are dozens of possibilities. Let's try not to judge."

It was easy to be angry. They were all on edge. Even Holden had been upset with Margaret. Emotions were running very high, and she had given the Blackburns a reason to circle ranks and turn their anger on the outsider.

Tim had never explained to any of them why he and his mom weren't close. She had attended Tim and Eve's wedding, but there had been so much going on that none of the Blackburns got a chance to talk to her in any depth. Tim rarely went home to Phoenix to visit. Eve had been there just once.

"I knew Tim was gone," Phoebe said, attempting to steer the conversation to something less divisive. "I didn't want it to be true, but I knew it was. I'm so sad about losing him. I'm going to miss him terribly."

"Me too," Wilder said. "Tim was one of ours, whether Margaret thinks so or not."

"We knew you didn't want to be right, Mom," Holden affirmed. "It must be upsetting to sense things like that before everyone else."

Luke was still listening. "So you actually had a dream

that let you know Tim had passed?" he asked. "Last night?"

"Yeah, I did." Phoebe looked forlorn, a reluctant receiver of the information. She didn't want any special powers or knowledge about life and death. She raised her hands and pulled gently on a lock of hair at the nape of her neck, twisting it around her fingers as she talked.

"If you don't mind my asking," Luke continued. "What was it like?"

"Nothing too elaborate," Phoebe replied. "It was just Tim there, telling me Eve was in danger. I didn't do anything to make it happen. I'm not sure I could have made it happen if I'd tried."

Luke looked interested. "How did you know he was… no longer alive? Did he say so?"

"No," Phoebe confirmed. "It's just that I've had dreams like that where people who have passed away come and talk to me shortly afterwards. It's never happened with anyone who is still alive. So…"

"That's impressive," Luke said. "Did Tim give you any information that might help us find Eve?"

"No, unfortunately not. I got the idea that it was urgent, though. A hurry. But no specifics."

Luke leaned back in his chair and pressed his fingers together at the tips. "You know, Phoebe, the Rosemary Run Police Department sometimes works with a psychic who consults on missing persons cases. I'm thinking maybe we should connect you with her. She's based in Sacramento. Her record isn't perfect, but it's good enough for me to consider her recommendations when she tells us she has something. Maybe she could help you connect with Tim again. Or with Eve. Or… I don't know, maybe you could connect with someone who has information about Eve."

"Like the old TV show, called *Medium*?" Phoebe asked.

"Sort of," Luke said. "I don't know how the psychic does what she does, but I figure it's worth a shot. Are you up for it?"

"Sure!" Wilder replied, answering for his wife. He grabbed her hand again, clutching it tightly. "Phoebe would be happy to try. Right, hon?"

"Right," Phoebe replied. "Whatever you think is best, Luke. I'll try anything if it might help us find Eve. It feels overwhelming to not have any solid leads. And with the snow storm supposedly coming tonight… I hope she's not out in the elements. I'm not exaggerating when I say I'll do *anything*. Anything at all."

"I know you will," Luke reassured.

He didn't seem to give any credence to Margaret's allegations. The Blackburns were relieved.

Holden nodded, resuming his leader-of-the-family duties. "Good. Then that's settled. Luke, do you have any more information on Eve? Even something small?"

"Nothing substantial," Luke replied. "I'm sorry I don't have more to report. But now that we know what happened to Tim, we can focus our efforts on Northern California. We know Eve made it to San Francisco. Our people are working on it. I promise you we're doing all we can."

"Is the forecast still calling for snow?" Holden asked. "I haven't checked for updates yet this morning."

"It is," Luke replied. "It's strange. The grass is green

and everything. I haven't been in Rosemary Run that long, but I didn't think we got snow."

"It's rare," Wilder replied. "I've been here all my life and I can count the times on one hand. They get plenty up on the mountain, but not usually down at this elevation."

"Do you think forecasters are mistaken?" Jake asked. "Maybe it won't happen."

"I don't know," Luke replied. "Meteorologists sound sure. I think we should plan for the worst and hope for the best. It's all I know to do. I'd sure like to find Eve before the winter weather gets here."

"If it's okay with you," Holden continued, not wishing to dwell on factors they couldn't control, "we'd like to ask for volunteers in the community and start spreading Eve's photo around." He was quiet for a moment. "We had hoped we'd be spreading Eve *and* Tim's photo. It's sad that it's just Eve now."

"I hear you," Luke said. "I can see that you folks cared about Tim. It's a shame, what happened to him."

The Blackburns agreed, nodding and shaking their heads, their faces hung low.

"If Eve saw the accident…" Phoebe began. "I shudder to think how that affected her."

"I know," Wilder echoed. "Unimaginable."

Luke closed his eyes, agreeing. It was hard on them all to absorb.

"As for spreading the word, yes," Luke replied, opening his eyes and determined to focus. "That would be helpful. Go to the media, too. Newspapers, TV stations… let's spread the word far and wide. I'll have our communications officer put together an official statement. What's your plan?"

Holden explained about going to the Internet, distributing posters, and making phone calls. He agreed that adding media outlets made sense. "Anything else you can think of?" he asked Luke when he was done.

"I think what you've mentioned will take all the time you have and will cover the most important bases," Luke confirmed. "You folks get busy. All except Phoebe, that is. I want her here with me to work with the psychic I mentioned. Let's keep in touch throughout the day. Call me right away if you find out anything even remotely new or useful."

"Will do," Holden replied.

"And Margaret…?" Phoebe asked.

"Try to put her out of your mind for now," Luke said. "I don't mean to sound harsh, but the grief counselor will take care of Margaret. We have to focus our energy on finding Eve. I want her found alive, and soon. As I know you all do, too. There will be time to make up with Margaret later."

20

E ve had blacked out once again. Her consciousness had failed her repeatedly, as had her grip on reality. She fought against her own mind. She didn't know how to help herself. Not really.

It was daylight now. Which day, she couldn't be sure.

Even though it was frightening to wake up not knowing where she was or what was happening, it was during those waking moments that Eve's happy memories comforted her.

She blinked her eyes gently as a memory of growing up at Brambleberry Fields came into view. Eve was there with her older brothers and their spunky Jack Russell Terrier named Scout. She had been no older than six or seven at the time, and she experienced the memory as if she were that young again.

Scout ran ahead of the Blackburn siblings in the grassy field, the dog feeling like a big animal despite the fact that he inhabited a small body. He always seemed larger than his physical form. He'd run right up to big dogs, sheep, and even horses as if he were in charge of them all. Eve remembered his feistiness, his white fur with big brown spots silky with water from morning dew on the grass, his eyes eager for adventure.

Life was simpler for Eve then, and not just because she was a child. Her disease had not yet manifested its evil presence. She was free, and clear. Her mind was her own. She hadn't yet disappointed anyone. She hadn't yet experienced the fear of what she might do to herself and those she loved.

Scout bounded through the grass in Eve's memory, followed closely by her big brothers. They were all faster than Eve, but they wouldn't leave her behind. Holden and Jake each held one of their sister's hands tightly as she ran her little legs as hard as she could to keep up. She remembered the thrill of moving so fast along with them. And she remembered looking up at Holden's face as he helped her. It had felt like she was flying, safely, under the watchful eye of brothers who loved her dearly.

She felt a pang of longing for that safety. She wondered if she'd ever have it again.

Next, a memory of Tim appeared front and center. It was the rehearsal dinner on the evening before their wedding. The event was held at a restaurant in downtown Rosemary Run called Honey Hog, a rustic-chic place with crisp white table linens set against exposed wood ceiling beams and red brick walls. The entire family had gathered, along with the bridesmaids and groomsmen.

Marrying Tim had been a dream come true for Eve. It was a dream that she hadn't been sure would ever come to fruition.

On the night of the rehearsal dinner, Eve felt especially grateful for her happiness and good fortune. She saw it all in her memory in rich detail. She could hear the gentle clinking of glasses after Holden gave a toast in his role as best man. She could see the fresh floral centerpieces on the table in front of her. They were baby blue forget-me-nots and white roses tied in bunches with sheer ribbon. Every element of the design was exactly as Eve had imagined. She again felt like the belle of the ball as she remembered.

She could smell the warm bread placed on the tables ahead of dinner. And she could taste the cake that was served for dessert.

As Eve remembered, she paid special attention to Tim's face. He looked so good to her in his suit and tie. He never dressed in suits for work, so it was a treat to see him wearing one for the special occasion. Eve watched him closely for any sign of nervousness or second thoughts. There were none. Tim smiled from ear to ear as he looked at her, his bride-to-be. His face was relaxed and happy. He looked like he was experiencing the same bliss that Eve was.

They had been truly content together. Their love was real.

Eve's thoughts shifted from the rehearsal-dinner memory to the baby she hoped she was now carrying. She wanted nothing more than for her baby to enjoy the same happy childhood that she had. Maybe she could live vicariously through her child and get a little piece of that happiness back for herself. Especially now that Tim was gone. He would want both of them to be happy.

There. She'd finally admitted it to herself. Tim was gone. He had died in Islamorada on their happy trip that was supposed to have been nothing but good. Eve was still reeling from the shock, but she was beginning to accept what had happened. But only beginning. It was all still fresh and new, even though it had happened days ago.

Eve had been nearby when Tim's jet ski was hit. She had been sunning herself on the beach and reading a novel on her smartphone. The novel was a romance about a winter trip to a tropical island, much like Islamorada. The story was getting good and Eve was thoroughly immersed in the characters, so she had opted to stay put and finish reading when Tim asked if she wanted to join him on a jet ski. Eve had never been on a jet ski, anyway, and wasn't sure she'd like it. She preferred slower, smoother rides, so she had told Tim she'd go kayaking with him instead. She urged him to go ahead and jet ski by himself.

They weren't scheduled to fly home for three more days. Plenty of time for finishing the novel. And for kayaking.

Now, Eve wondered if she had played a part in what happened.

If she had been on the jet ski with Tim, they would have been going slower. The collision with the boat wouldn't have been as violent. Also, if Eve had been on the jet ski, she would have seen the boat approaching and could have warned Tim to steer out of its way. Or maybe they wouldn't have been as far from the beach to begin with, and therefore not in the path of the boat.

Surely, Eve could have done something. At least, that's

what she told herself. She moved through a list of what-ifs, working her way slowly from denial to some semblance of acceptance.

If she hadn't been so wrapped up in the damn book, she could have suggested they rent kayaks right then, skipping the jet ski entirely. Kayaks would have been kept closer to shore. In fact, there was a quiet cove across the road on the Gulf side of the island. No boats entered, and they could have kayaked there.

If they hadn't been so slow getting out of bed and to breakfast that morning, they would have been eating lunch when the accident happened. They would have been safely tucked into a restaurant dining room instead of at the beach and in the water.

If they had gone to the History of Diving Museum like the concierge at the resort suggested, they would have been indoors and safely out of the water that afternoon. They could have been wandering hand-in-hand through SCUBA and diving equipment and talking about where they'd eat dinner that evening.

If they had taken a day trip to Key West like they'd considered, they wouldn't have been in Islamorada that afternoon at all. They could have been safely touring the Hemingway House or the keeper's quarters at the Key West Lighthouse. They would have been nearly two hours away from the boat that took Tim's life.

If they had chosen to vacation in Cabo like they initially planned instead of the Keys, Tim would have been on the other side of North America, far from that boat and the accident that harmed him.

There were a million possibilities. A million different

choices that would have kept Tim safe. The fact that he was in exactly the right place at the right time to be struck and killed by that boat seemed incredibly cruel to Eve. Tim could have swerved even slightly or deviated his path for just one minute, and he'd be alive right now.

It wasn't fair. In fact, it was insanely unfair.

Eve wondered, sincerely curious, how something like this could happen. Tim was a good, kind man. One of the best Eve had ever known. He didn't deserve this. Not that anyone did, but especially not Tim. How could it have happened? Why did it happen? Of all the ways the accident could have been avoided, why? She wanted answers.

Answers wouldn't bring Tim back, but Eve thought they might help her cope. They might be a comfort to her baby someday. The child would eventually want to know what had happened to his or her father. It was only natural.

For a long time, it had been hard for Eve to believe that she deserved a man like Tim.

He was handsome, and strong. He was well liked by virtually everyone who knew him. He was intelligent, more so than many people could begin to comprehend. And he used his brilliant mind for good. Tim cared deeply about the environment. He had chosen to spend his life using science to restore and renew the Earth. He had fallen in love with Northern California before he had even met Eve. He felt passionate about protecting the region's beautiful land.

You could see that passion in Tim's eyes. He was a quiet guy, shy and reserved. But if you got him talking about the environment, it was hard to shut him up. Other people could feel his enthusiasm. It was infectious. It was one of the things that Eve was most proud of about him.

But it was more than just his good looks, intelligence, and passion. During the inevitable times when Eve felt low, Tim's emotional stability worried her. He didn't have the ups and downs that she did. Instead, he maintained an even keel.

At first, Eve feared Tim would grow tired of her mental health challenges. She feared that he would leave her for someone more like him. Someone who didn't rely on medication for their wellbeing.

As for her own plight, Eve had gone as far as to think about what might happen to her if she were in a situation where she couldn't take her medication on schedule. She felt vulnerable due to her dependence on the chemicals. If she ever found herself lost in the woods, for instance, she wondered how quickly her mind would unravel. Or if there was a storm and medication couldn't be delivered to the pharmacy, she thought about how she would make it through.

Eve's therapist was a gentle woman with long blonde hair named Dr. Elaine Hubert. Their therapeutic relationship had begun when Eve's symptoms first manifested. Eve had been a teenager then, still in high school, while Elaine was a newly minted graduate of the PhD program at UCLA. She had grown up in a neighboring town by the bay, so jumped on the opportunity when a mental health services group in Rosemary Run had been looking for an additional practitioner.

Working in conjunction with a psychiatrist who prescribed the meds, Elaine had done a wonderful job getting Eve on top of her bipolar disorder. So well, in fact, that Eve had been able to attend college in Los Angeles herself and return with a bachelor's degree to show for her efforts.

Since Eve had been stabilized, and had completed several years of cognitive-behavioral talk therapy, she only saw Elaine once every quarter to check in.

But Elaine had given Eve strict instructions to call her if she ever had trouble. Elaine had also warned Eve that stopping her medication suddenly could cause symptoms to resurge, possibly worse than they had before treatment.

As Eve lay in the daylight, blinking her eyes and reminiscing, she thought about calling Elaine now. Elaine wouldn't be judgmental like Eve's parents and brothers. She'd want to help. And she'd understand what Eve was feeling.

If only Eve could remember how to get in touch with her. Elaine's number had been saved in Eve's smartphone, which was lost days ago.

Eve thought maybe she could borrow Saul's phone.

Oh, Saul.

She had forgotten about him for a moment. She had forgotten what had happened to him. It was a tragedy, the same as Tim's death.

Eve thought maybe she had been bad luck for the two men. Maybe both of their deaths were her fault.

Eve decided she'd try to reach Elaine and ask what she thought. She looked around the room, working to focus her attention and her eyes on the present moment. She'd need to use Saul's phone.

She found herself on the familiar brown couch, but Eve couldn't remember how she got there. She had been on the floor, last she knew. She had been beside Saul's body. That was until her mind had played tricks on her, Saul's face being replaced by Tim's.

Eve rolled over to face the living room. She steeled herself for the sight of Saul's body on the floor, vomit piled up beside his head. She knew it would be hard to see again.

To her great surprise, the floor was empty. And it was clean. Eve rose up on one elbow and scanned her surroundings. Everything was orderly. Saul's body wasn't anywhere to be found.

Within a few hours after leaving the police station, Holden's search party was in full swing. As planned, he had set up a headquarters at Tim and Eve's house. By lunch time, the place was buzzing with activity. Volunteers had answered the call to action. Their cars filled the driveway and hugged the curb in front of several houses in either direction.

Each of the Blackburns had their assignments. They were following directions to the letter. Lorelei and Imogen were keeping the kids busy as promised, and the staff members at Brambleberry Fields were holding down the fort and preparing for the inclement weather. Everyone was doing their part. It was a group effort, from a top-notch group.

Holden was in his element. He was a good leader. He wanted more than anything to help his sister and to help the rest of his family by bringing Eve home safely. He knew how to lead efficiently, and he put all of his leadership experience and skills to use for the search.

Margaret and Phoebe were still at the station, leaving the Blackburn men to their duties.

The guys stopped only briefly to eat food donated and delivered by Brick House Cafe. When management had heard about Tim and Eve's plight and learned that they had met in the cafe a couple of years prior, they refused to accept payment for lunch. They insisted that providing food for the volunteers was the least they could do.

To the Blackburns' relief, local media had responded positively to their request for coverage. Media outlets wanted to do everything they could to get the word out about Eve, and they immediately got busy scheduling interviews and gathering information.

One of the TV news affiliates out of Sacramento was the first to arrive at Tim and Eve's house. A pretty African-American reporter dressed to the nines and in full makeup knocked on the front door with a camera crew in tow just as Holden was finishing his turkey sandwich. She knocked hard, the sound echoing throughout the house.

"Knock, knock," Holden said. "She's here. And early. That's got to be a good sign."

Wilder and Jake chewed the last bites of their food, wiping the corners of their mouths with napkins and following Holden to the front door.

Ty and Marcus were away downtown distributing fliers.

The eldest Blackburn men put on their best welcoming smiles as they opened the door and led the news crew inside. They showed them to Eve's office where the cameramen set down their things and unpacked their equipment.

"Hi, I'm Sharonda Vinson," the reporter said. "Pleased to meet you. I'm just sorry it isn't under better circumstances."

"Thank you," Holden said. "We're getting a lot of that sentiment. And we appreciate it. We're just glad you're here."

The same news station had done a feature on Brambleberry Fields a few years back, but that was before Sharonda worked there. She had come from Milwaukee, and Holden figured she had probably still been in Wisconsin when a different reporter came out to the resort. He wondered if Sharonda had done any research on the family and their business.

"We're glad you called," Sharonda said, placing a hand on Wilder's arm. He must have looked like he needed a bit of comfort. "Mr. Blackburn," Sharonda said, addressing Wilder directly. "I have three kids of my own. I can only imagine what you're going through. I'm so sorry."

Wilder sniffled as he tilted his head back, trying to hold in his emotions. He had been doing okay until Sharonda mentioned her kids.

It was odd how random things could catch them off guard. The distress about Eve's disappearance and Tim's death seemed to come in waves.

"That's nice of you to say," Wilder replied to Sharonda. "I hope the story you air will help us find my daughter and bring her home. I surely want this story to have a happy ending."

"Me too," Sharonda confirmed. "How about we get started right away?"

"Sure," Holden replied. "What do you need?"

"To begin, I'd like to walk around the house and determine the best spot to set up cameras for an interview. Is that okay with you?"

"Yes, make yourself at home," Holden replied.

"And if you don't mind," Sharonda continued. "I'd like to get some footage of family photos and mementos around the house. We want to appeal to viewers' emotions. If they connect on an emotional level, they're more likely to take action that will help Eve be found. Do I have your permission to film items we find here in the home?"

Holden looked at Wilder to confirm.

"I'm sensing hesitation," Sharonda said. She was quick. Nothing got by her and she moved along efficiently.

Holden shrugged, deferring to his dad.

"It's just that Tim's mother, Margaret Fischer, may have some legal say in what happens with Tim's things," Wilder explained. "And she's not here. Last we saw her, a few hours ago, the detectives at the police station were taking her to speak with a grief counselor."

"Ah, I see," Sharonda mused. "I understand your hesitancy, but given the situation, I don't think we should wait. If one or both of you are willing to sign a waiver, that will suffice. I'm sure Margaret would want everything possible done to help her daughter-in-law."

Holden shrugged again, then looked out a window.

"What now?" Sharonda asked.

Again, Wilder spoke.

"Margaret wasn't in the best of spirits, last we saw her," he explained. "In fact, she seemed to have hostility towards Eve."

"Yeah, that's an understatement," Jake added.

Holden shot him a look that said to be quiet.

Jake was new to this, but Holden had dealt with the media before. He knew how things could get twisted around in an attempt to garner higher ratings. Sharonda seemed nice enough, but Holden didn't want the story to become about a squabble between the two families. That might make for interesting TV, but it wouldn't paint the family in a good light. It also wouldn't help bring back Eve.

This was a story about Eve being missing and Tim being killed, and nothing more. Holden wouldn't let his family's situation turn into a public drama.

Sharonda narrowed her eyes, considering. She made her decision quickly and moved on. "It's fine," she said. She reached into her bag and pulled out a waiver. It was already typed up with details that included permission to film inside Tim and Eve's house. Both Holden and Wilder signed as instructed.

Once the paperwork was out of the way, Holden and Wilder led Sharonda around the house. Two of her cameramen followed behind. Each time Sharonda saw something she thought might play well on film, she pointed it out. Most of the things she found useful were personal items. Deemed most compelling were photos from Tim and Eve's wedding, a dish on top of their bedroom dresser with some of Eve's monogrammed jewelry, and her pink silk robe that hung on a hook behind the bathroom door.

"Do you think showing this personal stuff will really help people connect?" Wilder asked. "Because it sort of seems like an invasion of privacy?"

Holden jumped in. "It will help, Dad. I know that much."

Wilder trusted his son. He gazed into Holden's eyes, searching for certain confirmation that they were doing the right thing. The Blackburn family had a responsibility to protect Eve's privacy since she wasn't able to do it for herself. Her mental health status made those concerns even more important.

"Okay," Wilder replied. "I suppose the good outweighs the bad here. This TV newscast will reach more people than making phone calls and handing out fliers ever could."

"Now you're framing this properly in your mind," Sharonda confirmed. "This newscast is a means to an end. Yes, we think about what our viewers want to learn and see, which is related to ratings. Ratings are, unfortunately, an inescapable part of what we do. But when a vulnerable individual like Eve is missing, our primary concern becomes how we can use the tools available to us to help find her. It becomes about community service. About humanity."

"Right," Wilder said.

"I know my audience," Sharonda continued. "Showing these personal items along with footage of you talking about how much you miss her will pull on their heartstrings. It will motivate them to remember Eve's face and think hard about whether they might have seen her recently. It will also motivate them to remain vigilant and watch for her. That's what we need... thousands of eyes and ears on the lookout."

Wilder nodded, accepting the process completely now. "Okay, I get it. Go ahead. Do whatever you need to do."

Sharonda motioned for her camera guys to do another sweep of the house, this time focusing on the items she referenced. They obliged, trotting dutifully, cameras on their shoulders and battery packs strapped to their waists.

She stood with Wilder and Holden while they waited for that portion of the filming to be complete.

Her earrings clanked against themselves and her bangle bracelets rattled every time she moved. Sharonda seemed out of place in the house. She looked ready for prime time, like she should be seated behind a news desk with a serious man in a suit and tie beside her. It was odd to observe.

When the cameramen were finished, they signaled to Sharonda.

"Okay," she began, speaking softly. "It's time for you to appear on camera. Are you up to the task?"

"Yes," Holden confirmed. "How many of us do you want to interview?"

Sharonda had already thought it through. "All family members who are here first. That's the two of you, plus Jake Blackburn, correct?"

"That's right," Holden said. "My mom is at the police station, and my younger brother is handing out fliers around town with his husband."

"Okay," she replied. "I'll want contact information for both of them. And for any other extended family. Where are your wife and kids, Holden?"

"They're home, and I'm sure they'd be happy to be interviewed."

"Good," she confirmed. "We'll see how much time we have, but I'll probably swing by."

"Jake's wife and kids would speak to you, too," Holden added. "And you can find Mom at the station. We all want to help. I can't say it enough."

Sharonda liked the sound of that. She continued, moving through her thoughts quickly. "And these volunteers… We'll want shots of them working. We will interview a few."

"Understood," Holden said.

"Anyone I'm missing?" Sharonda asked. "Margaret?"

Holden looked at his dad again. Wilder sighed.

"Whatever you think is best," Wilder offered. "We can give you her mobile phone number if you'd like to track her down. She might be found at the police station with Phoebe."

"Phoebe is your wife?"

"Oh, sorry. Yeah, Phoebe is my wife."

"I'm going to need notes on all of these names. Please be sure I get that before I leave. Holden, maybe you could jot that information down while I interview your father?"

Holden agreed and left to find paper.

Sharonda led Wilder to a chair in the living room that she had apparently thought had the best backdrop and natural lighting. Three large cameras were already set up on tripods, each with a cameraman to operate the equipment.

Once Wilder was settled in a comfortable position, an assistant placed a mic on the lapel of his shirt, then powdered his nose and forehead.

With flawless presentation, Sharonda spoke into the

camera, describing Tim's horrific death and Eve's vulnerabilities. She sounded so eloquent, so compelling, and so official that Wilder dissolved into a blubbering mess, right there as the cameras rolled. Everyone in Northern California would witness it within hours.

Sharonda said the footage would be shown on the evening news as the top story, along with carefully constructed interviews of other family members and volunteers. She implored Wilder to trust her and her team. She told him how she thought this feature had a good chance of helping Eve get back home. Maybe even before the sun should rise on a new day.

"You think it will snow?" Wilder asked Sharonda as he and Holden walked her to the door, unsure if the weather would impact her getting the story on the air. He suddenly felt like this news story was their only hope. A feeling of desperation arrived suddenly and threatened to overtake him.

"I don't know," Sharonda replied. "But I'll get this piece together before it does. You have my word. You'll see it on the five o'clock news. Featured story."

"Godspeed, Ms. Vinson," Wilder said, placing one hand on his heart as he said goodbye. "Godspeed."

22

Phoebe sat huddled in an uncomfortable black chair outside Luke's office as she waited for Minerva Ellery to arrive from Sacramento. She wondered what it would be like to work with a real psychic. She hoped she wouldn't be wasting precious time.

Luke had given Phoebe a stack of glossy home and garden magazines to read. She had scoffed until he explained that staying calm and relaxed seemed to help Minerva with her process. Phoebe had reluctantly agreed.

The Blackburn matriarch was flipping through an article about backyard chickens when Pamela walked over to tell her that Minerva had called and was due to arrive shortly.

Phoebe thanked the woman, but she had a hard time making her voice sound anything other than devastated about the state of her life, in general.

Phoebe wished she could be back at the family's resort with nothing more to worry about than which was the

most environmentally friendly chicken coop for Greta
Garbo and Marilyn Monroe. She wished Eve could be
there too, typing productively in her office and sipping
coffee out of her favorite Hello Kitty mug, Tim safely at
his place of employment.

She wondered how things had gone so wrong. She
thought about how it wasn't even remotely fair. Phoebe
knew that if Eve was alive and in her right mind, she'd be
thinking the exact same thing. Fairness was a topic that
had come up time and again during Eve's therapy with
Elaine.

Phoebe sat up straight, remembering Elaine for the
first time since all of this had happened. She wasn't sure
how she could have forgotten, but she made a mental note
to call Eve's psychologist just as soon as she was finished
talking dreams and psychic abilities with Minerva. Phoebe
wasn't sure if there was anything Elaine could do, at least
not until Eve was found. But Phoebe thought it seemed
important to let her know what was going on.

Neil stopped to chat as he was walking back to his
desk, presumably having finished with Margaret and the
grief counselor. He sat down in a chair beside Phoebe and
crossed his arms over his chest.

Neil was a handsome man, much like the men in the
Blackburn family.

Phoebe remembered the buzz around town when he'd
met and fallen in love with his wife, Cate. Her first
husband had been killed less than a week before the two
of them were seen around Rosemary Run having obvious
feelings for each other. To make matters worse, Neil had

been investigating the first husband's murder, and Cate had initially been a suspect. It was quite the controversy in certain circles. But Phoebe also remembered the genuine affection Neil and Cate clearly had for each other from the beginning. The more time that had passed, the easier it was to see they belonged together. Most people had come around to their side, eventually.

No one can deny true love. Not for long.

"How are you holding up?" Neil asked.

"Oh, fine and dandy," Phoebe replied, doing her best to fake a smile. "How did things go with Margaret?"

Neil sighed, biting his bottom lip. His eyes seemed sad, like a puppy dog's. As Phoebe looked at him, she thought that he really did care about the people he encountered in his line of work. She thought it was probably rare to find investigators as caring as Neil and Luke.

"Margaret is grieving," he said. "And right now, she's angry."

"I can understand that," Phoebe replied. "Especially since Tim and Margaret didn't have the closest relationship."

"You aren't kidding," Neil added. "We always think we'll have more time to mend old wounds. But it doesn't always happen that way."

"Don't I know it," Phoebe mumbled.

Neil was talking to her more casually than Luke had. Phoebe knew Neil better. The two of them had known each other longer.

"Hey," he said. "I know you're worried about Eve. I don't know how things will play out, but I know that you're an amazing mother to her. You shouldn't have any doubt in your mind about that. Your daughter loves you. That much is certain."

Phoebe let her head lean gently on Neil's shoulder. He reminded her so much of her own sons. "I hope you're right," she said. "I've tried to be a good parent."

"And you've succeeded. You're a model for the rest of us."

Phoebe admired the way Neil had taken Cate's kids in and loved them as his own. They'd suffered a terrible, unexpected loss when their father died. Neil was well aware that he could never replace Mick Brady, but he had become an irreplaceable addition to the Brady kids' lives.

"That's sweet," Phoebe said. "But we see what kind of dad you are. I'd say you're the model parent around here."

Neil chuckled. "Then suffice to say it takes one to know one."

Phoebe agreed. She sat back up, lifting her head from his shoulder, figuring she should rally and muster her strength for Minerva.

"Neil," she began, "are you aware of what happened when Eve was a teenager? The… incident? Because you and I didn't know each other back then. I want you to…"

He sighed, choosing his words carefully. "I wasn't on the force then, but I've read through the case files. And I've heard from some people who were around when the incident took place."

"I'd like you to know about it," Phoebe said.

"I'm not sure it's relevant, other than to help us understand Eve's particular difficulties."

"I agree," Phoebe confirmed. "But I've been trying to hide the story for so long that I think I might feel better if I put it completely out in the open. It's a heavy burden to carry… The shame, that is…"

"It wasn't your fault," Neil said softly, his voice barely audible over the background noise from the busy station.

"I can't help but feel like it was… It is."

"I don't see it that way," Neil reassured.

"She's my daughter," Phoebe mused. "I brought her into this world… defective. How am I not responsible? And I can't fix her. For all the rest of her life— assuming she is found safe— she'll need to be watched over closely. She'll need to remain on medication. Every single day. We were lucky that she had Tim. He was a Godsend for us all. But what are the odds that she finds a love like that again? Not very high, I imagine. And… Wilder and I… we'll grow old." Phoebe began to cry as she talked. "We won't be able to take care of her for as long as she'll need it. What's a parent in that situation supposed to do?"

"Oh, Phoebe," Neil said. "I hear you. It's sad. And hard. But defective is a harsh word. I don't think it's helpful to think of it that way. These things happen."

"But it goes against the ways of the natural world, you know?" she continued. "Parents are supposed to raise kids who can care for themselves completely when the parents are old… and die. Not to mention, it's nice when the kids can take care of the parents in their final years. Thank God we have three sons who will hopefully do that."

"Not hopefully. They will. Holden, Jake, and Ty love you and Wilder— and Eve— fiercely. You are a close family. It's obvious to everyone who knows you." Neil placed a hand on Phoebe's shoulder as he continued with his pep talk. "In fact, I'd wager that the boys would watch over Eve after you're gone, should the timelines work out that way."

"Maybe…" Phoebe replied. "But they shouldn't have to. All three of my boys have kids of their own."

Neil turned in his chair to face Phoebe squarely. "You've got to reframe that whole thing in your mind," he said. "Life is messy. It's sometimes horrible. But it's sometimes beautiful. And that's what makes it worth living. There's no perfect scenario. Believe me, I know from experience. If someone had told me I'd fall in love with a woman in Cate's position, and then quickly become a step-dad to three grieving kids, I never would have believed them. I mean, I was a bachelor, living in a little house with my dog and going to work every day. I spent my spare time reading fiction. Or watching TV. These days, I'm taking kiddos to sports practice, helping with homework, and comforting them when they cry about missing their dad. And you know what, Phoebe?"

"What?"

"I wouldn't trade it for anything. I'm exhausted. I'm stressed. But I'm happy with the good. I take the bad along with it. I'm sure you do the same in your own life… with Eve. Everything feels harder right now. I promise, you will get through this."

Phoebe smiled, a fresh tear in her eye. "You're right. I don't mean to sound so sad and dramatic."

"No apology necessary," Neil affirmed. He patted her shoulder. "I'm here to listen to whatever you want to tell me… including what happened when Eve was a teenager. Okay?"

Before Phoebe could answer, she saw Pamela heading their way with a pretty brunette following closely behind.

"Mrs. Blackburn," Pamela announced. "Meet Ms. Minerva Ellery."

23

"Hello, Phoebe Blackburn, is it?" Minerva said as she reached a sun-tanned hand out.

Minerva appeared to be in her late thirties, younger than Phoebe but older than her kids. Her nails were clean and painted a subtle shade of peach, but that was the only thing subtle about her. At least, as compared to the way women typically dressed in Rosemary Run.

Minerva looked every bit the part of a witchy woman in a flowing, faded brown dress with long sleeves and buttons all the way up and down the front. The hemline nearly reached to the floor, but thanks to undone buttons from mid-thigh down, the fabric flowed behind Minerva's calves as she walked. Underneath, she wore leather, knee-high gladiator sandals with crisscrossed straps, and apparently not much else. Phoebe could see Minerva's nipples protruding through the thin fabric across her braless chest. Adornments to top off the look included bangle bracelets, hoop earrings, and a necklace with a large hemp-leaf pendant dangling down into her exposed cleavage. Minerva's long, wavy brown hair danced around her shoulders and stretched all the way to her waist.

Phoebe gave Neil a look as if to ask if he was serious. He returned her gaze with an expression that said he was, indeed.

"What?" Minerva asked. "Am I not what you pictured?"

"Oh," Phoebe began, working to collect herself. "It doesn't matter what you look like, right?"

Minerva cocked her head and looked quizzically at Neil. He jumped in to help Phoebe save face.

Phoebe was a beautiful woman herself, but Minerva oozed sex appeal, and Neil suspected it was rattling for Phoebe to encounter under these circumstances. Neil thought maybe he and Luke should tell Minerva to consider toning it down a little next time.

"Phoebe has had a long couple of days," Neil inserted. "As Luke probably told you on the phone…"

"Nope," Minerva said, holding up a sun-kissed finger to stop him.

She looked to Phoebe like she had just returned from a tropical island. Where she cast spells. And maybe even lured sailors with her enchanting music and singing voice to shipwreck on a rocky coast.

"Don't tell me," Minerva continued. "I don't want to know anything. It interferes. Better for me to go in blind."

"Okay," Neil said. "I do remember that now, from the last case you consulted on. My apologies."

"No one needs to apologize," Minerva emphasized. "Let's just get started. You called me here for an important case. And I dropped everything to make the trip. Let's do what we're here to do, friends. Sound like a plan?"

Phoebe nodded, perplexed by the woman, but eager to see if she might help.

Neil led them to a small room at the back of the station that looked like it used to be someone's office. "In here," he said. "No one will bother you. I'll make sure of that."

"You aren't staying?" Phoebe asked.

"I thought I'd send Pamela in to record the session," Neil replied. "I'm better used on other aspects of the investigation. But I'll be around. If you get anything, I'll be right back to hear all about it. I promise."

Phoebe half-smiled, growing nervous.

"Relax," Minerva said. "I don't bite. I promise."

"Okay, then," Phoebe replied. "Pamela will be great. We're good."

Neil closed the door softly. Less than a minute later, Pamela arrived as promised, recorder in hand.

When all three ladies were seated and ready, Minerva began.

She had brought a large bag with her. Phoebe almost expected the strange woman to pull out a cauldron and various witch's brew ingredients. Instead, Minerva retrieved a recording device of her own, a CD player, and a sketchpad and pencil.

"What's all of this for?" Phoebe asked. "Or I guess I should ask... How does this work?"

Pamela pushed the record button and gave a thumbs up to let Minerva know she could proceed, on record.

"There's no set way that it works," Minerva explained.

"Strange as that sounds, it's different for me almost every time."

"Okay," Phoebe replied.

"The recording Pamela is making will be for police department records," Minerva continued. "But I like to have my own. Sometimes, I get additional information from thoughts or dreams or instincts after sessions like this, and it helps to be able to refer back to everything that was covered."

"I understand that," Phoebe replied. "Luke decided to connect us because of a dream I had…"

"Wait!" Minerva said, holding up that finger again. "I know you're eager to tell me your story, but I need you to wait. I don't want what you tell me to act as a suggestion that steers my mind one way or another. Interpreting my psychic abilities is difficult enough without those types of suggestions. So please, wait until I ask."

"Alright," Phoebe said sheepishly. She was way out of her element and just wanted to get on with things.

"This CD player holds a disk with meditation music on it that helps me get into the right frame of mind. It's Tibetan music, with singing bowls and rushing water in the background. I can't explain why, but it seems to get things flowing for me. If it bothers you, I have headphones I can put on."

"It won't bother me," Phoebe confirmed.

"As for the sketchpad and pencil," Minerva explained. "Much like the music, it helps with my flow. I've found if I just let my hands sketch things that I see, it helps get them out of my mind."

"So, you see things, like in your mind's eye?"

"Yeah, I do," Minerva confirmed. "I also hear things. And sometimes, it's as if a package of information is dropped into my brain. I can then sort of unfold that package and interpret it. It isn't an exact science. Over the years, I've developed certain symbols that whatever higher power's sending me this information seem to use. For example, when I see a white rose, it means that someone has passed on."

"Wow," Phoebe mused, fiddling with the edge of one shirt sleeve. "Do you think this information comes from a higher power?"

Minerva readjusted her long hair, flipping a section of it behind her shoulder. "I can only guess," she explained. "But something is working in conjunction with my mind. Like I said, I can't explain it. Which reminds me... Before we get started, I should warn you. I don't always interpret things correctly. I don't want you to place hopes on what I say and then I turn out to be wrong."

Pamela closed her eyes and nodded as Minerva said this. She seemed to appreciate the woman's transparency.

"Okay," Phoebe agreed. "But Luke said maybe you could help me connect and interpret symbols I see. Is that accurate?"

"Maybe. Let's take it one step at a time. Do you happen to have anything that belonged to the person who is missing? And... Don't tell me who it is. I don't want a name or relation to you. But if you have something that belongs to him or her, it may help if I hold it in my hand."

Phoebe thought about the contents of her purse. She hadn't been prepared for such a request. "Oh!" she exclaimed as something came to mind. "Keys! I have—

the person's— keys." She was careful not to use the pronoun *her*.

"Perfect!" Minerva replied. "Keys are especially good because we hold them in our hands. Objects we hold repeatedly soak up the energy that radiates from our solar plexus out to our hands."

"Great!" Phoebe said. She didn't understand what Minerva was talking about exactly, but she was happy to have pleased her.

Phoebe was loosening up now and was feeling more comfortable with Minerva. She was also gaining confidence about her own part in this process.

She was especially glad that she had Eve's keys. It was a stroke of luck, really. Phoebe had almost tossed them into the bowl beside Eve's front door when she left the house that morning, but something told her to hang onto them because she might need them later.

Minerva closed her eyes and took the keys from Phoebe's hands, careful not to look at them. Phoebe realized what Minerva was doing, and why. The only key ring Eve had was a flat silver piece with her initials monogrammed on the front. Eve loved monograms and had them all over the place. Other than feeling the cursive font, Minerva probably wouldn't be able to tell whether the keys belonged to a man or a woman.

Minerva kept her eyes closed as she moved the hand with the keys out to one side of her body. With her free hand, she picked up the pencil and held it over the blank page on the sketchpad. "Pamela?" she asked. "Would you start my CD, please? I kind of got ahead of myself."

Pamela did as Minerva asked without speaking. She

was there to record what happened and nothing more. She was being diligent about not interfering.

Soon after Pamela pressed play, the sound of a babbling brook filled the room, followed by a series of chimes from singing bowls. The music was ethereal. It immediately slowed Phoebe's heart rate and made her want to close her eyes along with Minerva.

Phoebe could sense a seriousness in the air. It felt like Minerva was really doing something.

"This music…" Minerva said softly. "It helps to open the third eye, cleanse the chakra, and enhance transcendental meditation."

"I'm sorry," Phoebe replied. "I know some of those words, but not all of them. You may need to explain in a little more depth."

"Later," Minerva said as her head swayed slowly with the beat.

"Okay," Phoebe replied, feeling like she might have spoken out of turn. She didn't want to interrupt.

"Quiet, please," Minerva asserted as she scribbled on the sketch pad.

Phoebe and Pamela watched as circles and letters seemed to pour out. This went on for several moments that felt longer than they actually were.

Phoebe kept an eye on a wall clock in the small room. It ticked its rhythm, plodding on and reminding her of the precious moments passing them by. They had to find Eve. Tim had communicated the urgency. It *had* to happen soon.

Finally, Minerva opened her eyes. She looked very sad, empathy on her face.

"What did you see?" Phoebe asked. "Is it E..."

Minerva grabbed Phoebe's hand and looked deeply into her soul. "You've already lost someone, haven't you?"

Without warning, a tidal wave of sadness about Tim's death poured over Phoebe. She had loved him like a son. She began to cry. Not just for the pain Eve had surely experienced seeing it happen, or for the anguish Tim must have gone through in the instant his spirit left his body. She cried for herself. She already missed Tim. She had grown close to him. And she knew that the longing for him to come back to them would only get worse.

Tears poured down Phoebe's face as she thought about how Tim had seamlessly integrated into the Blackburn family, as if he had always been a part of them.

She would miss seeing him in his Phoenix Suns cap and the silly boat shoes he liked to wear on weekends. She'd miss their discussions about the local watershed and how to protect the rare grasses that grow down near the bay. And she'd miss seeing the smile on his face every time her daughter walked into the room.

"I'm sorry," Phoebe mouthed. "It's painful."

"Take your time," Minerva replied.

Phoebe was beginning to like her now. Minerva was genuine, if a bit unusual.

"You're right. I've already lost someone."

"A son," Minerva added.

Phoebe nodded, not bothering to correct Tim's status to son-in-law. Son was accurate enough.

"And someone else you love is in danger."

"I think so, yes," Phoebe barked between sobs.

"A daughter."

"Yes."

Minerva gripped Phoebe's hand tightly. "It isn't too late for her," she pleaded. "I believe she's still alive."

Phoebe's body heaved with relief at hearing this. She surprised herself by how much she believed what Minerva was saying. Logic told her that Minerva had no way to know for sure, but instincts told her Minerva was right.

"And the dream you mentioned…" Minerva continued. "The son told you about the danger to the daughter."

"Yes, I…"

"You knew he had passed before you received confirmation in waking life," she affirmed.

"Yes!" Phoebe said, getting excited now. She thought maybe this meant that specific information about Eve was coming next. The more Minerva got right, the more hope Phoebe placed in her.

"And the burning questions center around how to find this daughter. Is her name something that starts with an E sound? Evie?" Minerva withdrew her hand from Phoebe's and scribbled the capital letter E on her sketchpad as she spoke, still holding the keys in the other hand. "Eva?"

Phoebe raised both hands to her face. She wondered if someone had told Minerva Eve's name. She was blown away. "Eve. My daughter's name is Eve." Minerva nodded knowingly. "Did someone tell you that?" Phoebe asked. "Luke? Did he mention her name?"

"No."

Phoebe thought it through. Eve's name hadn't been on the news yet. "Social media?" she asked Minerva.

"No, I haven't been online since last night."

"Tell me more," Phoebe implored. "You're on the right track."

"Alright," Minerva confirmed. "I get the idea the son's death was an accident. I'm seeing my symbol for a timeout, which is what I see when a life ends suddenly but no one is at fault."

"That's right."

"Is Eve handicapped? Or is something wrong with her physically? Because I see the shape of a woman seated. That's my symbol for a wheelchair or a handicap of some sort."

"Not physically," Phoebe confirmed. "Mentally. We think she's off her meds due to the trauma she experienced when her husband was killed last week."

"I see," Minerva continued, closing her eyes again, still sketching. "And a baby? I see a baby."

"Oh, my God," Phoebe blurted. "They were trying to conceive. That's another reason I suspect she might be off her meds. Are you saying…?"

"I don't know for sure, but that's what I'm seeing."

"Wow."

Minerva tilted her head again, as if the motion helped the gears turn inside her head. "I see your daughter in a safe place, but I don't think she realizes it. I think the danger is what she might do to herself. I think she's in a bad place, mentally. A very bad place."

"That's what I'm afraid of," Phoebe affirmed.

24

Phoebe cried as she drove, all the way back to Tim and Eve's house. It was mid-afternoon, and the sense that time was running out grew stronger by the minute.

The wind had picked up and temperatures were continuing to drop. The snow that had been forecasted was coming, sleet already pelting the ground. It looked odd falling on green grass and plants. The entire day seemed bizarre, like something out of a bad movie. It hardly felt real to Phoebe, except for the terror and the pain that had overtaken her body. Those feelings were all *too* real.

Minerva hadn't been able to tell her anything much beyond what she already knew: that Eve was in danger and they needed to find her fast. When Phoebe had pressed Minerva for a location, the woman had come up empty. She had told Phoebe to trust her own instincts, but to get out there looking, and fast. She promised to keep working on it and to call the detectives if she received any additional information.

Minerva had seemed to be legitimate, at least. Phoebe couldn't come up with any other explanation as to how she knew what she did.

As Phoebe walked in the door, she made a beeline for Wilder. He was seated at the table alongside a handful of volunteers, talking on the phone. She forced his arms open and pressed herself against his chest.

"I need to call you back..." he said into the receiver, pressing the button to hang up before waiting on a response. "What is it, honey? Come here. I've got you."

Phoebe continued to cry, unable to stop herself. Wilder stood up and guided his wife into a bedroom where they could have some privacy. He closed and locked the door behind them, then climbed onto the bed.

"Lay down with me," Wilder said. "I'll hold you."

"I... Eve is out there..." Phoebe mumbled. "I can't just lie down in bed."

"Shh," Wilder said, wrapping his arms around his wife and stroking her hair. "There are dozens, if not hundreds, of people working to find Eve right now. You can rest."

Phoebe continued to sob, her eyes puffy and red. She'd never cried so hard in her life. "Aren't you going to ask me what happened with the psychic?"

"Why, sure," Wilder confirmed. "What happened with the psychic? How was she?"

"Strange, but nice," Phoebe said. "She knew things that were right. But she didn't know where we could find Eve. All she could tell me was to trust my instincts."

"Did you tell her about your dream?"

"Yeah, and she didn't tell me anything about how to reconnect with Tim," Phoebe explained. "I'm beyond exhausted. I'm frazzled. I can't begin to know what to do with myself. And we're running out of time. Minerva—the psychic— thinks Eve is in a bad mental space and in danger of harming herself. I think so too."

"Phoebe, hon," Wilder said gently. "I don't know anything for sure right now, but maybe the best thing you could do is go to sleep. Maybe Tim will return to you and tell you where we can find her…"

Phoebe looked at her husband, desperation thick like fog around them both.

"I'm serious," Wilder confirmed. "How about you take a rest? I'll watch over things and wake you up the minute anything big happens. I promise."

"I am really tired," Phoebe sobbed. "Bone tired."

"Then rest. Maybe ask Tim to come talk to you in a dream? It's worth a shot, don't you think?"

"Will you stay here at the house? Near me?" she asked. "I don't want to be away from you right now. I'm not sure I can do this by myself, Wilder. I need you."

"I'll be right here. Trust me. You have my word."

"Okay," Phoebe said reluctantly, slipping under the covers and adjusting a soft pillow under her head. "But… the snow?" she said, her level of alarm rising again.

"I know," Wilder said. "We'll get through it. I'll keep watch. You rest."

And she did.

Phoebe fell peacefully asleep, pausing just long enough to ask Tim to come and talk to her. It was a long shot, and way outside of what Phoebe or Wilder ever thought they'd be doing. But it felt like the thing to do. They had to try.

25

When she had realized Saul's body wasn't on the floor, it sent Eve into a full-blown panic.

As she sat up and looked around again, she felt the strange tingly feeling like she sometimes did when she was coming out of an anxiety attack. She couldn't be sure if her panic was on the rise, or if the peak had already come and was on its way down.

Day blurred into night. Eve had no idea what day it was or how long she'd been at Saul's house.

She still couldn't trust her own mind. And she hated herself for her body's failings.

But Eve knew what she had seen. It was all vivid in her mind. Right here, beside this brown couch, Saul was dead. The vomit. Their dance. Their party. The sex. The whiskey. And the heroin. She remembered it all.

So, what if she had made some bad decisions? It wasn't her fault that Saul was dead.

Or was it?

Eve reached for her hair like she did when she was

anxious. She began smoothing it, then pulling it, so hard that she ripped strands from her scalp.

Think. Where is the body?

She wondered if she had moved it and then forgotten.

No, she knew she hadn't. She wasn't sure she was strong enough to move a grown man's dead body, anyway.

The sound of sleet on the window startled Eve. It took a minute for her to realize what the sound was. She didn't think she'd ever heard of sleet in Rosemary Run. Only on vacations with her family to snowy winter places, like Lake Tahoe. The thought of frozen precipitation falling from the sky in the here and now scared her. It seemed out of place. Unnatural.

Did it snow in Rosemary Run?

Eve didn't think so.

She was sure that she was in her hometown of Rosemary Run. She remembered Wingman's Pub, then going back to Saul's place. But what if her mind had been playing tricks on her then? What if she wasn't in Rosemary Run at all?

Where am I? Has someone taken me? Have I been… kidnapped?

Eve's heart beat hard in her chest like a bass drum, a shrill ringing sound filling her ears and making a harsh cacophony.

She pulled her knees to her chest and rocked back and forth as she retraced her steps. Her body odor was growing more and more pungent. Eve scarcely noticed it.

Think. Think!

She remembered the flight from Florida. Tim had purchased tickets from Miami into San Francisco because they were the least expensive. He had said the drive to and from the airports would be fun. Part of their adventure. But the flight back to California hadn't been an adventure at all. Not without Tim. Eve had slept on the plane, her head pressed awkwardly against the wall beside her window seat. She had been in such shock from Tim's death that she could barely focus minute to minute.

She was still numb.

What happened next? Before Wingman's Pub? How did I get there?

Eve balled her hands into fists and slammed them against her temples. She was angry with her mind for withholding important information. It was in there somewhere. It had to be.

She screamed. A long, loud sound that came from the depths of her. Beating her temples harder and harder, she yelled, then cried. Then yelled some more. The anger burned inside of her like hot lava. Her veins seemed to carry piping hot liquid. Her blood felt like it was boiling.

"It's okay," a woman's voice said.

Eve jumped, then pulled her knees in tighter.

Who is that?

"Who's there?" Eve asked timidly.

"I'm a friend," the woman said, the outline of her figure coming into view.

Eve couldn't make out details, but she could tell the woman was tall and thin. She had shoulder-length hair that curled at the ends. Eve didn't respond, instead trying to determine whether the woman was real or a figment of her imagination.

"How are you feeling, Eve?"

How does she know my name?

Eve squinted at the woman as she came closer. She could make out more now. Black hair. Red lipstick. Close to her own age.

Staying quiet, Eve looked at the woman curiously.

"I'm glad you're awake. Is there anyone I can call for you? Your family maybe?"

What is this woman talking about? Just like Saul, wanting me to call someone. I can't call my family.

"No," Eve admonished, pulling at her red hair. "No, no, no."

"It's okay," the woman said again. "Stay calm. You're okay."

This banter was making Eve angrier. She resented being told what to do.

Is she real?

"I know you told Saul to think of you as Eve Smith, but I'd love to know your real last name," the woman said.

Eve's eyes widened, like a deer in headlights.

She knows Saul?

The red-lipped woman persisted. "I told you, I'm a friend. You can talk openly to me. I already know what happened between you and Saul."

A hand shot up to Eve's mouth, terror coursing through her. "What do you know?" she mumbled.

"He told me everything you talked about. I'm up to speed."

Oh, no. I'm in trouble.

"Who… Where…?" Eve stammered.

She knew Saul was dead. But she couldn't quite

determine if this woman was real. She cursed her faulty mind once more.

Think, dammit.

"He couldn't be here today, so I came instead," the woman added.

"Who are you?" Eve asked. "Wait. *Elaine?* Is that you? Did you change your hair?"

"No, sorry. I'm Nell."

"Nell?" Eve replied, growing more confused by the minute.

"Nell Caraway. Pleased to meet you."

Nell stepped closer to Eve and extended a hand for her to shake, but Eve turned away, refusing.

"Is Elaine someone in your family?" Nell asked. "Can I call her for you?"

Eve raised her eyebrows at this. She had thought about calling Elaine. But she didn't know her therapist's number. And Eve had lost her phone. She quickly dismissed the idea. She had bigger problems to deal with.

"No."

"Okay, then," Nell said. "How about something to drink?"

Hell, no. I will not party with this woman. Look what happened to Saul.

"No drinks," Eve said.

"No problem," Nell replied. "Saul told me you had dinner together last night."

We did. Wait…

A bolt of lightning went through Eve as the impact of Nell's line of questioning settled over her.

She's testing me. Trying to catch me in a lie.

"Eve, I was thinking it might be time to call the police to see if they can help you find your way home. Saul thought it would be a good idea."

Struggling to make sense out of what was happening, Eve descended into paranoia. She suddenly felt like Nell would blame her for Saul's death. And turn her into the police.

The bloody knife. The drugs. The vomit. Saul's dead body. Tim's dead body.

It all swirled in Eve's head like a horrible, bad dream that she couldn't wake up from. Whoever this Nell was, Eve didn't trust her. Not for a minute.

Eve thought back to what had happened when she was a teenager. How that boy, Josh Tolbot, had died. And police had blamed Eve. She certainly didn't want to go through that again. She had disappointed so many people. And Josh... he lost his life. The two of them had been depressed and suicidal together, commiserating with each other.

Misery loves company.

They had even made a suicide pact. They would meet on the roof of one of Rosemary Run's tallest buildings downtown, the one that housed Decker's Department Store. They'd jump together, flying like free birds through the air until it all came to an end. All the suffering. All the pain. It would all be over.

Eve remembered the day like it was yesterday. It was winter, dreary and gray. In fact, the anniversary was coming up soon.

She could still remember Josh's goofy smile as he talked about how he'd feel moving through the air like a bird. He had even talked Eve into getting matching bird tattoos on their wrists. They'd skipped high school and had gone all the way to Sacramento that morning to get the ink. Using simple black lines, the tattoo artist had added a single bird in flight to each of their left wrists.

Eve looked down at her wrist as she remembered, the tattoo faded but still there. Her mom had suggested she get it removed, but Elaine thought Eve should keep it as a reminder of her own strength. She had lived, after all.

Closing her eyes now, the memory washed over Eve. She could see Josh looking over the edge, then smiling back at her as she prepared to step up on the ledge with him. He had been her first boyfriend. Her first love. And her first time making love. She remembered taking his warm hand and stepping up beside him, the hard pavement of the sidewalk looming below.

She remembered their countdown. She remembered how— at the last second— her parents had burst through the door to the roof, crying and calling her name, horror on their faces. Eve had hesitated as she turned to look at them, while Josh jumped.

Tears came to Eve's eyes as she remembered the horrible thud Josh's body made as it hit the sidewalk. She remembered being arrested, the cold handcuffs hurting her wrist where it was still sore from the tattoo. She remembered the look on Josh's mom's face as she spit and said it was all Eve's fault.

I've got to get out of here. Nell thinks I killed Saul.

Frantic, Eve began scanning the room for an exit.

I can't let them get me.

She knew she had to leave. She didn't know where she

was or where she would go, but there wasn't time to worry about that now. Eve simply had to get out.

Eve stood and like a frantic animal, ran towards the sliding doors on the far side of the room. They led outside, she was sure of it.

"Wait!" Nell called. "It's cold out there..."

Slowing down long enough to open the doors this time instead of slamming into them, Eve made her way out into the bitter, wintry weather wearing nothing but the clothes on her back. She didn't have a coat. Or shoes. Or her purse and what little contents remained inside that might have reminded her of her old life.

The air burned as it entered Eve's lungs.

She wrapped her arms around herself as tightly as she could, then ran through the cold, wet grass.

26

At five o'clock, Wilder, Holden, and Jake gathered in Tim and Eve's living room alongside a slew of volunteers. Everyone had stopped what they were doing to watch Sharonda's story on the evening news.

Phoebe was still sleeping hard, so Wilder let her be. He knew the news segment would be uploaded to the station's social media accounts shortly after it aired, and a volunteer had offered to get a rough recording by holding up her smartphone in front of the TV.

Sleet was turning to snow outside, and it pelted the windows furiously. Several volunteers remarked how strange it was to see the winter weather in Rosemary Run, falling on green grass, no less.

Wilder, Holden, and Jake knew that the weather meant more dangerous conditions for Eve. They tried not to dwell on it. They were doing everything they could. After the news, they planned to check in with Luke and Neil to find out if there had been any new developments.

The familiar tones that accompanied the evening news

rang out from the television, and a hush fell over the house. The mood was somber, but hopeful.

As promised, Sharonda had succeeded in making sure the Blackburns' story aired first. She and her male co-anchor looked sincerely concerned as a picture of Tim and Eve occupied the space between them on the screen.

Sharonda opened by saying that she had spent the afternoon in Rosemary Run with the family, then her cohort explained Tim's tragic death. A network affiliate in Florida had apparently assisted, because they cut to an interview with Roger Wilson in Islamorada, the wooden sign for the Keys Cove Resort and Marina in view behind him.

Seeing Roger and the resort sent a jolt through the Blackburn men. It had been one thing to hear about the place and talk to Roger on the phone. It was quite another to see the man and the place with their own eyes. It brought a fresh wave of sadness for everything Tim and Eve had been through.

Sharonda quickly shifted the focus to the search for Eve, a compelling b-roll compilation of mementos from the house playing beside her as she spoke. She looked into the camera and explained that Eve was a vulnerable adult who was suspected of being off her medication. She pleaded with viewers to be on the lookout for the young woman, then played the interview where Wilder had cried.

"Look at that sorry son-of-a-bitch," Wilder mumbled when he saw himself on screen.

"Come now, Dad," Holden said. "You did well. It's moving."

Jake nodded to confirm, and Wilder seemed appeased.

A series of additional interviews played through the television, followed by the tip line for the Rosemary Run Police Department, just as Sharonda said they would. It was well done, without a doubt. The piece lasted more than five minutes. For evening news, the Blackburns knew that was an eternity. Sharonda had done right by them.

"That should help a lot," Holden said. "Thank God."

"I think so, too," Jake added. "Now, we need to get right back at it. Everyone we talk to should be reminded that we're referring to the same story Sharonda covered on the news. Let's really drive that home."

"You're exactly right," Holden added. "We want to keep top of mind presence, as they say in marketing. We want people thinking about Eve at all times until she's found and brought home."

"I'll give Ty a call and make sure he and Marcus know to mention it as they hand out fliers," Jake offered.

"Good," Holden said, crossing his arms over his chest as the three of them stood up to get busy again. "And see if they need warmer clothes. Or a break. Coffee, maybe. They must be cold out there."

"Will do," Jake confirmed, then left the room.

It was less than five minutes until he came back, a look of distress on his face. Holden and Wilder were standing and looking out the window at the snow as they talked about next steps.

"What's wrong?" Holden asked his brother, seeing his alarm.

"Is it… Eve…?" Wilder asked.

It seemed like he had to muster his courage before he could speak his daughter's name. He wanted to know. And he also didn't.

"No," Jake said.

"Then what?"

"It's… Margaret, I guess."

"What do you mean?" Holden asked. "Is she okay?"

"I just got a text from Victoria," Jake explained, looking perplexed. "I think Margaret is okay, yes. But Victoria says she turned on us."

Wilder winced. "I was afraid of this. She was itching to take her anger out on us."

"What did Victoria say?" Holden asked.

The three of them looked at each other for a long, heavy moment. They could guess. They knew how Margaret could hurt them if she really wanted to.

"She says Margaret went to the other news station in Sacramento. They just aired a piece opposite Sharonda's that wasn't... as flattering."

"Right," Holden said, biting a knuckle and resisting the urge to punch the wall next to him. "Dammit."

They rushed to the computer Jake had been using in Eve's home office and hurriedly searched for the clip. It was there. The headline made their heart sink:

Rosemary Run Suicide-Pact Woman Strikes Again. Husband Found Dead in the Florida Keys.

The three of them felt sick as Jake pushed play and they braced for what was to come. They knew it wouldn't be conducive to creating good feelings for Eve. Quite the contrary. This might actually impede the search process.

A female-male anchor team appeared just like

Sharonda's had, only this pair looked angry instead of concerned. They introduced the story by immediately showing footage of Margaret in tears outside the police station as she clasped framed photos of Tim in her arthritic hands. She was shivering, pale, and her hair was a disheveled mess. It was obvious she was purposely being made to appear feeble.

"How low," Jake muttered as he paced at the back of the room. "I can't believe it. Except, I can. Tim wouldn't want this. I know that much for sure."

Wilder raised a hand to quiet his son so they could hear the rest.

As the news piece continued, Margaret talked about how she had just learned her son was killed, days after the fact, without having been informed by his wife who knew almost an entire week prior.

"That's not fair," Jake shouted. "Come on!"

"Quiet," Wilder said, watching, his own anger rising in his chest.

After a brief silence on screen as Margaret was shown crying and clinging to the photos, the anchors returned and flashed Eve's mugshot. It was from the time she had been arrested as a teenager, after Josh Tolbot had died by suicide. Eve looked bewildered in the mugshot, her eyes hollow and empty. It had been just weeks before she received a diagnosis and was prescribed the medication that had allowed her to achieve stability and to lead a relatively normal life.

"Those evil… Assholes," Wilder said under his breath. "All of them. Pure evil."

The anchors described what had happened the day

Josh died, then showed footage of Margaret saying she didn't think her son's death was an accident. She continued, talking about how disturbed Eve was, and going as far as to say that she thought Eve had encouraged Tim to put himself in harm's way, just like she had with Josh.

The piece concluded with the anchors asking viewers to contact the Rosemary Run Police Department if they had any information that would bring Eve to justice, specifically mentioning foul play leading to Tim's death.

Holden sat stunned, speechless. Jake continued to pace the floor.

Wilder slammed his fist down hard on the desk, in a rare expression of physicality. "How dare they?" he asked. "Of all the lowdown, dirty things to do…"

"We have to figure out how this happened," Holden said.

"How what happened?" Phoebe asked, rubbing her bleary eyes as she entered the room. "Is it Eve? Has she been found?" Her voice escalated with each word.

"No, Mom," Holden said. "I'm afraid not. We've had a… complication with the media coverage of Eve's disappearance, that's all."

"Okay," Phoebe said skeptically.

Wilder shook his head as if he could shake some of the frustration out. "Nothing that can't be handled, my dear," he said, taking his wife's hand and then wrapping an arm around her waist. "You look like you have something to say."

"I do," Phoebe replied. "I had another dream. It was Tim."

"Really?" Wilder asked, excited. "Tell us! Did he tell you how we can find her?"

"It was strange," Phoebe explained. "He didn't say, exactly, but as I looked at him I got a feeling… a knowing… I'm not sure if it was Tim telling me or not."

"And?" Wilder asked.

"She's in the snow… nearby," Phoebe continued. "And she's still in grave danger. Out of her right mind. But I think we will get a phone call this evening that will let us know where to search. When it comes, we must be ready to move quickly. We need to gather a group of people who are willing to help search, on foot."

27

Without waiting, Wilder, Phoebe, and Holden, drove to the police station.

They wanted to speak to Luke and Neil. And they wanted to be ready when the call came in. They knew the call Phoebe sensed would probably be directed to the police station rather than to them personally.

Big, fluffy flakes of snow fell on the windshield of Holden's SUV. The sun had set, and it was nearly dark outside.

Jake stayed behind at the house to rally the volunteers and coordinate a search party willing to get out in the cold, snowy weather.

They didn't say it out loud, but after seeing Margaret's anger spewed publicly in Eve's direction, Wilder, Holden, and Jake were afraid some volunteers would turn against them and refuse to help. It was a harsh reality of human nature. Not to mention, a harsh reality of how easily things could get twisted in the media.

Margaret's statements on camera had been mostly

true, but they were shrouded in misunderstandings and exaggerations. The news station had apparently believed her without bothering to learn the other side of the story. Or worse, they just wanted the ratings. Producers had to have known that their coverage was far more inflammatory than Sharonda's.

Sharonda's treatment of the story had been ethical. And responsible. It was a shame all reporters and media professionals couldn't hold themselves to the same standard.

Wilder handed Phoebe the news clips to watch on his smartphone as they drove. First Sharonda's, then the other one. Phoebe remained strong as she watched, comforted by her dream and the thought of the call that would lead them to Eve. Her strength impressed them all. Many mothers would have fallen apart in Phoebe's situation.

When they walked into the police station, the place was bustling more than ever. Pamela looked tired, but she was still bobbing around, conversing with officers and answering phones.

"Oh, good!" she exclaimed when she saw the Blackburns. "You're back. Luke wants to talk to you. Follow me."

They did as they were told, weaving around desks as they made their way to Luke's office. Phoebe thanked Pam, who winked in return.

Maybe there was good news.

Luke greeted them with a similarly enthusiastic response. "Come in, folks," he said with a cautious smile. "We have a break."

Phoebe's legs nearly collapsed under her upon hearing this.

"Did you find our girl?" Wilder asked.

He hadn't mentioned it to anyone, but Wilder had been experiencing chest pain all afternoon. He thought it was likely due to stress. He wondered how much more he could take before having to go to the emergency room. The last thing he wanted was to be out of commission when his family needed him most.

"Not yet, but I think we're close," Luke confirmed. "Just a few minutes ago, I received a call from a peer counselor named Saul Milton. He works with a new crisis center that's affiliated with Berryhill Community Medical Center, down by the bay."

"Okay?" Phoebe asked eagerly, slapping Wilder's knee.

"The call," Holden said. "There it is."

Luke continued without stopping to ask what they were referring to.

"Saul is on his way here right now to make a statement. The crisis center he works with is sectioned into apartments where patients can detox or rest in a calming environment. Eve was found without ID on Sunday evening and shuffled through the hospital system, eventually landing in the crisis center. She was a Jane Doe. She wouldn't tell them her name. She didn't have a phone or ID on her. Staff members finally figured it out thanks to Sharonda's news piece."

"I knew the news would do it," Wilder said. "Oh, thank God."

"They initially thought Eve was an addict," Luke continued. "Apparently, she's been out of it much of the time. And she's been suffering from hallucinations. Saul stayed with Eve until another peer counselor named Nell Caraway took over this afternoon."

"So, they have her?" Phoebe probed.

"That's the thing," Luke said. "A little while ago, she ran out of the center and disappeared."

"Into the snow?" Holden asked, incredulous. "She'll freeze to death."

"We have officers en route as we speak," Luke said. "They'll search the area. She couldn't have gotten far on foot. Saul tells me she wasn't wearing a coat or shoes when she left. *They'll find her.*"

"I'll call Jake," Holden added. "He can get some volunteers down there to help. Should they gather at the crisis center?"

"Yes. That's good," Luke said. "Please do. Neil and James are already on their way. Tell Jake to look for them when he gets there. And yes, at the crisis center. It's a block south of the hospital."

"Tell them to be careful on the roads," Phoebe said. "It's slick out there. The last thing we need is someone else in harm's way."

"Will do," Holden said, then stepped out of the room to make the call.

"You should be proud of yourselves right now," Luke said to Phoebe and Wilder. "That newscast made all the difference."

"Did you see Margaret on the other station?" Wilder asked.

"I did," Luke confirmed. "And I'm not concerned with that just yet. We don't suspect any foul play in Tim's death. Like I said earlier, Margaret is grieving. I'm sorry you folks are getting the brunt of her anger. But let's focus on finding Eve."

"Right," Wilder agreed. "I had planned to talk to you about offering a reward for information on her whereabouts, but it looks like there's no need."

"Yeah, I'd wait," Luke confirmed. "It may not be necessary."

As they talked, Minerva burst through the door of Luke's office, her long hair trailing behind her and bouncing like she was in a shampoo commercial.

"I've got something!" she said.

Phoebe jumped up and hugged Minerva, who had added leggings, boots, and a coat to her siren outfit. "I got something, too!" Phoebe exclaimed, then quickly introduced Wilder.

"What is it?" Luke asked, picking up a pen, ready to take notes.

"I was driving, and it just washed over me. I had stopped to eat before heading back to home, but then the snow started falling. Anyway, I saw Eve alive. And I sensed a large body of water nearby. I think it was the bay."

Phoebe nearly jumped up and down upon hearing this additional confirmation. "Go on," she said.

"I saw her very cold, out in this weather. I think she's in danger of freezing. And she's still a danger to herself. She isn't in her right mind."

Wilder exhaled loudly.

"I know," Minerva continued. "It's scary. I'm sorry to spring this on you. I imagine it's hard to absorb. But I saw her in my mind's eye, huddling underneath a long row of tall trees all planted in an even, straight line. There were boats in the distance. A marina."

Luke picked up the phone receiver on his desk and began dialing. "Yes, this is Detective Luke Hemming," he said when the person on the other end answered. "We have reason to believe our missing person is near the Sweet Balm Marina. Focus the search there, looking carefully underneath the row of tall trees on the property. I'm on my way. Oh… And get in touch with Saul Milton. Tell him to meet us there instead of at the station."

28

———

Luke tore out of the parking lot, blaring the lights and sirens on his unmarked police vehicle. Snow fell hard through the air, and was beginning to stick to the ground. Holden followed, driving his own SUV as his parents and Minerva rode along. They had all practically ran out of the building.

Holden had received nothing more than a hasty introduction to Minerva and instructions to update Jake.

"Someone want to tell me what's going on?" Holden asked after he sent a quick text to Jake. He didn't usually text while driving, but decided this situation warranted taking the risk. "Did another lead come in?"

Phoebe explained, telling Holden she and Minerva had connected that afternoon, as well as about her dream where Tim appeared again. Then Minerva filled in from her perspective, including the information she had received about Eve being near the marina.

"Luke apparently knew exactly the place Minerva

described," Phoebe said. "He made a phone call to focus the search there, and we're on our way."

"Wow," Holden said. "I'm impressed, Mom. You and Minerva should work together again sometime."

Wilder nodded, the pain in his chest increasing. He didn't have the energy to say much. He didn't want anyone to know he was hurting. He figured it was due to the additional stress. He willed the pain to go away, telling himself he'd get it checked out as soon as Eve was safe and sound.

The drive to the bay took less than half an hour. Wilder dozed along the way.

When they pulled into the parking lot at Sweet Balm Marina, Neil and James were there to greet them. A slew of uniformed officers were combing the woods near the waterfront, along with even more people in plainclothes who were apparently volunteers.

The energy of action filled the air. It was a hopeful energy. But also a cautious one.

Temperatures were below freezing. Eve had been in the elements for a while now. Unless she had somehow found shelter, she'd be facing frostbite. Or worse. Not to mention, if she was suicidal, the cold, deep bay was a looming hazard.

Before Luke and Holden had even parked their vehicles, Jake's Jeep pulled in behind them, followed by a string of volunteer vehicles filled to the brim with people who wanted to help. Everyone shuffled out eagerly, ready to get down to business. No one spoke as they powered on flashlights, zipped up coats, and tucked their ears into warm hats.

Neil came rushing over to quickly greet the Blackburns and update his partner, nodding his thanks to Minerva. "We have all hands on deck here, folks. If she's out there, we'll find her."

"Is the K9 unit here yet?" Luke asked.

Phoebe bristled at the idea. "You're sending a dog to search for our daughter?" she asked as she stepped out into the cold.

"Yes," Neil confirmed. "Two K9 units are en route. They'll be here any minute. That's a good thing, Phoebe, I promise."

"Aren't the dogs for… you know?"

"Cadavers?" Minerva asked, stepping out from the back door behind Phoebe. She didn't have nearly the filter the Blackburns were used to.

Phoebe winced at the word. "Yes…"

Neil walked over, facing Phoebe and placing both hands on her shoulders. "Look," he said gently. "The situation is volatile. I won't pretend it isn't. And this could go either way. I hope we find Eve alive. But we're here to find her, no matter what her condition. If you like, you can wait in a car with the heat on. That way, you can be near the action without having to be right in the middle of it. There's no shame in that. This is your child, after all. I'd probably wait in the car if it were one of mine."

Phoebe looked at Wilder, who seemed distant. "I don't know," she said.

"Mom, I think that's a good idea," Holden affirmed, zipping his own jacket and pulling gloves over his big hands. "How about you and Dad stay here, at least for a little while? We'll let you know the minute we find something."

"I'll stay with you," Minerva offered.

"Wilder, hon?" Phoebe asked, turning to her husband who was still seated in the back seat of Holden's SUV. "Should we wait here?"

Wilder nodded, breathing deeply to hide his discomfort.

"Okay," Phoebe agreed. "Get us the minute you find anything. Promise?"

"I promise," Neil said. "Now, stay warm."

Phoebe and Minerva got back into the SUV with Wilder while the others headed towards the action. The K9 units pulled into the parking lot, dogs and handlers bounding out of their cars to the rescue at top speed.

Phoebe thought it remarkable how some people run towards a disaster with unmitigated courage. She wondered what the world would do without those people. She was proud of her sons for being those people.

As she peered out the window, she saw Ty arrive, then get out and follow the others towards the trees, joining his older brothers. Marcus trotted closely behind.

Before long, Phoebe began to see other people she knew arriving, too, their warm breath visible in the cold air, their faces sincere and eager to help.

Pamela was there. So was Robert, the grief counselor. But it wasn't just police department personnel. Lorelei arrived to join the search with Holden. Mona was there with some other neighbors. As was Victoria. And Elaine. People were coming from all over Rosemary Run to help.

Phoebe recognized people she knew from stores and restaurants around town.

Jake had done a beautiful job of rallying the community. And no one mentioned Margaret or the accusations she had volleyed during her news interview. Apparently, the Rosemary Run community saw that for what it was: a devastated mother grieving the loss of her only son, and experiencing anger. They didn't think any less of Eve. Or any of the Blackburns. *They understood.*

Emotion welling up in Phoebe's throat, she got out of the SUV to take part. The others gave her courage.

"I have to go," Phoebe said to Minerva and Wilder.

"I'll go with you," Minerva chirped. "Should we wake your husband?"

Phoebe glanced at Wilder, his head slumped forward onto his chest. "No, if he's asleep, we should let him rest," she said. "He kept watch while I took a nap this afternoon. We've both been exhausted by all of this. It's my turn. I'll update him when we return."

"Okay," Minerva said, stepping out and bundling up.

The ladies— becoming fast friends— joined the group, collective body heat warming them all on this cold, snowy night.

Phoebe soon met Saul and Nell, hugging their necks and thanking them for watching over her precious Eve like they had.

When that conversation was finished, Phoebe was surprised and delighted to see a caravan full of dozens of Brambleberry Fields employees parking and getting out of their vehicles. They had even brought Freckles, the farm dog, along to do his part.

"Oh, you dear ones," Phoebe said as she greeted them, tears flowing. She leaned down to let Freckles lick the side of her face and scratch him behind the ear.

"We had to close because of the weather," one of Jake's assistants said. "The road over the mountain is shut down. We figured it was more important to be here, anyway. With you. Our family."

Phoebe felt the love surrounding her. She had the best life. The best people. She scolded herself for having wallowed in despair earlier. She never should have complained about having a daughter with a mental illness. The truth was, she'd never trade Eve in a million years. And the challenges surrounding Eve's illness could be handled with the support of a loving community.

In a flash, Phoebe knew that Eve was going to be found alive that night. Any minute, in fact. She couldn't explain how, but she knew her daughter would be okay. They'd get her back on her medication. Elaine would see Eve in therapy more often, perhaps recommending time in an inpatient facility. The Blackburn family would help Eve grieve Tim's death. They'd find a way to make up with Margaret. Everything would be okay.

Minerva grabbed Phoebe's hand, giving it a squeeze. "It's happening. She's here. And she's alright," Minerva whispered in Phoebe's ear. "Do you feel it?"

Phoebe nodded her understanding. "I do." She smiled, happiness and relief filling her entire being.

"Any minute now," Minerva said, echoing Phoebe's thoughts, a matching smile on her face.

Back at Holden's SUV, Wilder was losing consciousness.

His chest tightened as the pain became nearly unbearable. It felt like an elephant was sitting squarely on top of him. His breath was short. He couldn't quite get a full breath, no matter how hard he tried.

He knew exactly what was happening. He had asked for this.

Wilder grabbed his phone clumsily out of his pocket to call someone. Anyone. But his hands were shaky and he dropped the device. It slid under the driver's seat, out of reach.

He tried to lean forward and position himself to reach beneath the seat, but his body wouldn't cooperate. He got as close as he could to the floor, but couldn't wedge his arm far enough underneath. He wasn't sure there was any way to reach from this position, even under normal circumstances.

He knew he'd have to step out of the vehicle and enter through the driver's seat if there was any hope of retrieving the phone. And he knew he couldn't do it.

Not now.

Not ever.

Wilder hadn't told a soul, but that morning while everyone was busy planning the day, he had gone into Tim and Eve's bedroom, then locked the door and talked to God.

He didn't consider himself a religious man, and he didn't claim to know much about how matters of life and death worked, but he believed in some kind of higher power. Determined to give Eve the best chance at survival and to give Phoebe the best chance at getting her child back, he had decided to appeal directly to that higher power and beg for his daughter's life.

Wilder had dropped to his knees beside the pair of windows, looking out and up to the heavens. He touched his thumbs to his index and middle fingers, like he did sometimes during meditation. Then he tilted his head back, closed his eyes, and pleaded his case out loud. The others had been too busy discussing the search to hear him.

He told God that he was an old man who had lived a wonderful life by any standard, and that he could not have asked for more. He'd enjoyed many years with the best wife on the planet, the two of them a perfect pairing. He'd lived long enough to know his children and to see them grow into productive adults, and he'd even made it long enough to meet his grandchildren. He thanked God for every single day of his life.

Wilder said he was ready to go if he had to, and he asked to trade his own life for Eve's. He asked that she be found safe, and that through therapy and with the love of her family, she eventually be made whole again.

He had said these things with the full intention of his spirit. He meant them wholeheartedly.

He had hoped his plea would be heard.

As Wilder Blackburn quietly slipped away from this life, rescue crews found Eve. She was out of sorts and confused, shivering while huddling against a tree near the marina, just like Minerva had said.

Eve was taken to the hospital by ambulance, Phoebe and Holden riding along with her while Jake, Ty, and Marcus followed closely behind. They rejoiced. They celebrated. Phoebe vowed not to leave her daughter's side.

Only later did they learn that their beloved Wilder had gone. He had left Phoebe a note explaining his plea. She read it while sitting on Eve's couch, with one arm around their daughter.

While Phoebe didn't consider herself religious and didn't claim to know how matters of life and death worked, she said a prayer of thanks to her beloved husband. If he'd had anything at all to do with Eve being found, she was grateful.

The Blackburns would move forward, taking the good with the bad and holding close the knowledge that life was messy. It was scary. And it was terribly unfair sometimes.

But it was also breathtakingly beautiful.

THE END.

———

Get the next book in the series:

Her Buried Secret
Rosemary Run - Book Five

———

BONUS CONTENT -

Extended Epilogue

Find out what happens to the Blackburn family ten years later in the FREE extended epilogue, available exclusively when you sign up for Kelly's email newsletter at kellyutt.com:

Her Darkest Hour - Extended Epilogue

Rosemary Run Short Story

Get a FREE prequel short story exclusively when you sign up for Kelly's email newsletter at kellyutt.com:

Her Troubled Mind

———

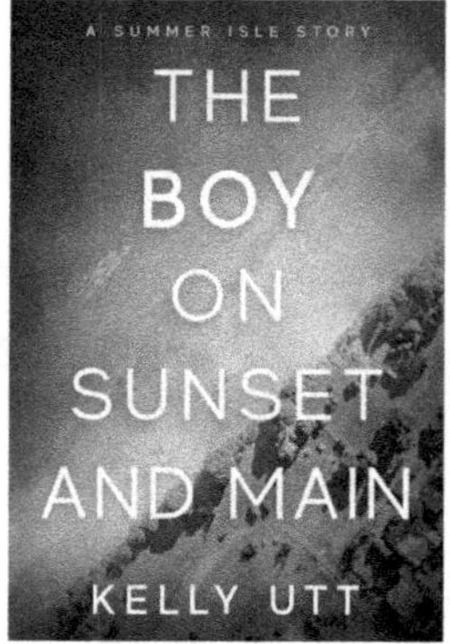

Sample Kelly's newest series, The Summer Isle, with a FREE prequel short story exclusively when you sign up for her email newsletter at kellyutt.com:

The Boy on Sunset and Main

ENJOY THIS BOOK?

A NOTE FROM AUTHOR KELLY UTT

Did you enjoy this book? You can make a big difference.

Reviews are the most powerful tools in my arsenal when it comes to getting attention for my books. As much as I'd like to, I don't have the financial muscle of a New York publisher. I can't take out full page ads in the newspaper or put posters on the subway.

(Not yet, anyway.)

But I do have something much more effective than that, and it's something that those publishers would kill to get their hands on.

A committed and loyal group of readers.

Honest reviews of my books help bring them to the attention of other readers.

If you've enjoyed this book, I would be very grateful if you could spend just five minutes leaving a review (it can be as short as you like) on the book's Amazon page and on Goodreads or BookBub.

Thank you very much.

ALSO BY KELLY UTT

Have you read them all?

——————

In the Rosemary Run Series

In the charming Northern California town of Rosemary Run, there's trouble brewing below the picture-perfect surface. Don't let the manicured lawns and stylish place settings fool you. Nothing is exactly as it seems. Secrets and lies threaten to upend the status quo and destroy lives when— not if— they're revealed.

SHORT STORY PREQUEL - HER TROUBLED MIND

Download it Free at Kelly's website: kellyutt.com

BOOK 1 - HER DEEPEST FEAR

BOOK 2 - HER HIDDEN PAST

BOOK 3 - HER BOLDEST LIE

BOOK 4 - HER DARKEST HOUR

BOOK 5 - HER BURIED SECRET

BOOK 6 - HER WORST MISTAKE

BOOK 7 - HER SILENT MISERY

In The Summer Isle Series

It's paradise on the sparkling tropical shores of Hideaway Isle, Florida. But despite postcard-worthy appearances, there's trouble lurking just beyond the sun, sand, and sea that promises to wreak havoc in this seemingly idyllic utopia.

With riveting turns that will leave you breathless, each Summer Isle novel features a deep dive into a different islander's story.

SHORT STORY PREQUEL - THE BOY ON SUNSET AND MAIN

Download it Free at Kelly's website: kellyutt.com

BOOK 1 - THE SISTERS OF KESTREL CAY

BOOK 2 - THE GIRL IN HIDEAWAY PARK

BOOK 3 - THE MAN AT NIMBUS MARINA

In The Past Life Series

The Past Life Series chronicles the Hartmann and Davies families across time and space. This life-affirming story, anchored by the deep affection between George and Alessandra, reveals how the connections we share can ground us during even the most difficult times as we endeavor to learn what we're made of.

Join the family you'll feel like you already know as, together, they explore the meaning of life beyond what lies on the surface and fight to keep each other safe.

SHORT STORY PREQUEL - WAIT FOR OUR TURN

Download it Free at Kelly's website: kellyutt.com

BOOK 1 - TELL ME I'M SAFE

BOOK 2 - SHOW ME THE DANGER

BOOK 3 - KEEP THEM FROM HARM

BOOK 4 - TAKE ME TO FIGHT

BOOK 5 - PICK UP THE PIECES

———

Be the first to know when new books are released by signing up for Kelly's e-mail list at www.kellyutt.com.

Kindle Unlimited Subscribers read for free.

ABOUT THE AUTHOR

STANDARDS OF STARLIGHT BOOKS
KELLY UTT

Kelly Utt writes emotional novels for readers who enjoy both suspense and sentimentality. She was born in Youngstown, Ohio in 1976.

Kelly grew up with a dad who would read a book on a weighty topic, ask her to read it, too, and then insist they discuss it together, igniting her passion for life's big questions. That passion is often reflected inKelly's novels, giving them a depth which leaves readers wanting more and thinking about her stories long after the last lines are read.

She holds a Bachelor's degree in psychology from the

University of Tennessee, Knoxville and she studied graduate-level interactive media at Quinnipiac University.

Kelly lives in the Nashville suburb of Franklin, Tennessee with her husband and sons.

www.kellyutt.com

www.ingramcontent.com/pod-product-compliance
Lightning Source LLC
Chambersburg PA
CBHW071258190726
48292CB00007B/2583